EDITORIAL REVIEWS OF
THE FRENCH EDITION

Narcisse on a Tightrope

Olivier Targowla

NARCISSE ON A TIGHTROPE

A Novel

Translated from the French by Paul Curtis Daw

DALKEY ARCHIVE PRESS

Dallas / Dublin

Originally published by Maurice Nadeau as *Narcisse sur un fil* in 1989

Copyright © by Olivier Targowla in 1989

Translation copyright © by Paul Curtis Daw, 2021

Introduction copyright © by Warren Motte, 2021

First Dalkey Archive edition, 2021

ISBN: 9781628973242

CIP Data available upon request

Dalkey Archive Press
Dallas / Dublin

Printed on permanent/durable acid-free paper
www.dalkeyarchive.com

Contents

Balancing Act
Warren Motte

OLIVIER TARGOWLA'S NAME will not be immediately familiar to most English-speaking readers. And indeed that is something they share with most readers in France. For despite the excellence of his writing, the indisputable originality of his vision, and the steadfastness with which he has pursued his literary career, Targowla has not achieved the kind of popular success that has gratified certain other writers of his generation. That may be due to a variety of considerations: the fact that the quicksilver quality of his books resists easy, conventional classification, for instance; or perhaps because he has not been as eager as some to become a media darling; or maybe it is because his novels have all appeared at the Éditions Maurice Nadeau, rather than one of the larger, more corporate Parisian publishing houses. Nadeau himself was quick to recognize Targowla's writerly potential—in itself no small testimony, for Maurice Nadeau (1911-2013) was a legendary figure in the French literary world, a man endowed with an extraordinary and nearly infallible nose for literary talent, who published and promoted people such as Louis-Ferdinand Céline, Nelly Sachs, Georges Bataille, Nathalie Sarraute, Jorge Luis Borges, Witold Gombrowicz, Fernando Arrabal, Tahar Ben Jelloun, and Georges Perec, among many others. Nadeau's reputation for boldness is abundantly evinced in the catalogue of the publishing house he founded; and it is thus all the more appropriate that Olivier Targowla has found a home at the Dalkey Archive Press, whose commitment to innovative, underivative fiction runs deep.

Born in 1945, Targowla worked for many years as a journalist. In the 1970s, he authored two books of nonfiction: *Les Médecins aux mains sales* (Doctors with Dirty Hands, 1976), on occupational health physicians, and *Deux Valises à Toulon* (Two Suitcases in Toulon, with Jean-Pierre Barou, 1979), which deals with a particularly grisly murder case in the south of France. He launched his career as a novelist in 1989 with *Narcisse sur un fil*, the book you now hold in your hands, in Paul Daw's superb, finely attentive English translation. You will not be disappointed, and after you finish reading it you will be eager to read more of Targowla's work. Five novels follow upon this one, each as excellent as the others, though none of them has been rendered into English as of this writing. *L'Homme ignoré* (The Unrecognized Man, 1990) puts on display an individual who resides insecurely, like many of Targowla's protagonists, on the margins of things. *La Peau de l'ombre* (Skin of Shadow, 1992) traces the life of a man who has lived for many years under a false identity, and who must now become himself again. *Distances* (1996) deals with the relations between a professional pianist and his dying mother. The playfully plaintive title of *Être un jour invité quelque part* (To Be Invited Somewhere, Someday, 2005) announces the story of an individual who is obliged to return to a place he had once called home, and where he now feels like an alien. *Un pas de côté (dans la rumeur du monde)* (A Step Aside [in the Babble of the World], 2011), Targowla's most recent novel, focuses on several different people who are called upon to rethink the way they are making their way through life, who grapple with circumstances both crushingly banal and utterly particular.

Narcisse on a Tightrope, as you will shortly discover, is a wonderfully distinctive novel. Its hero is Narcisse Dièze. His name is powerfully cratylic, for he spends a great deal of his time and his energy in close introspection, and he is clearly a bit off-key (the word *dièse* in French designates a musical flat). Or perhaps more than a bit, actually, insofar as he has spent the last seventeen years of his life in a psychiatric hospital. His internment there has not been as otiose as one might imagine, however, for he has fathered thirty-five children (or seventy-two, or one hundred and seventy-one, depending upon who is counting) upon the exceptionally complaisant nurses who have worked there over the years. Despite his brief, serial relationships with those nurses, Narcisse remains an exquisitely peripheral figure, a loner who has never figured out where he might fit in any of the communities he has been able to glimpse, however distantly. His difference is his most familiar trait; his inadaptation to the simplest situations is conspicuous; and his bumblings are constant and unrelieved. He's a beautiful loser, he's a schlemiel. And in that perspective, even though Narcisse is absolutely idiosyncratic with regard to everyone else he meets, it might be argued that he takes his place in a venerable cultural lineage including precursor figures like Adelbert von Chamisso's Peter Schlemiel, Ivan Goncharov's Oblomov, Italo Svevo's Zeno, Henri Michaux's Plume, Jaroslav Hašek's Good Soldier Švejk, James Thurber's Walter Mitty, Isaac Bashevis Singer's Gimpel, Samuel Beckett's Watt, Saul Bellow's Herzog, Philip Roth's Portnoy, Heinrich Böll's Hans Schneir, and Bernard Malamud's Fidelman, to name just a few. Like those noble individuals, Narcisse is constitutionally benighted. He dramatizes his ineptitude for all to see, in a performance that is fundamentally ludic, and at times comic. In broad focus, he acts out a special kind of critique upon traditional notions of heroism; in close focus he performs just for us, holding a funhouse mirror up to us and daring us to recognize ourselves therein, carnivalizing our struggles, forebodings, joys, and ways of being in the world.

Olivier Targowla's novel is as eccentric as its hero—and I say that in high admiration. It is quirky and unpredictable; it is suavely suggestive; it is lapidary. Targowla practices a minimalist style throughout, one which he will refine still further in his other novels. It should be recalled that French writers came to minimalism a bit later than their American counterparts. Those latter writers—one thinks of people like Raymond Carver, Ann Beattie, Frederick Barthelme, Mary Robison, Tobias Wolff, and Nicholson Baker—were heavily influenced by experiments in the plastic arts and (to a lesser degree) in music. That inter-art influence was undoubtedly less pronounced in France, when young writers such as Jean-Philippe Toussaint, Marie Redonnet, Jean Echenoz, Annie Ernaux, and Pierre Michon began to try their hand at minimalist expression in the 1980s. Yet they could nevertheless lay stake to a tendency in their own national tradition in ways largely unavailable to American writers, pointing to the striking terseness of French neoclassical writers like Pascal, La Rochefoucauld, La Fontaine, and La Bruyère, or to the stylistic sparseness of certain more recent figures like Albert Camus, Maurice Blanchot, Nathalie Sarraute, and Samuel Beckett.

The French writers of Targowla's generation practiced minimalism in strikingly different manners, but they shared a fundamental concern for the health of the literary culture they inherited from their elders. Jean-François Lyotard had famously declared the bankruptcy of the "grand narratives" in his *Postmodern Condition: A Report on Knowledge* (1979). Therein, he captured and articulated (just as John Barth had done across the Atlantic, in his 1967 essay "The Literature of Exhaustion") the spirit of the age. Or *one* of the spirits of the age, in any case, manifesting itself in an anxiety centered upon the limits and possibilities of literature. Faced with a significantly reconfigured cultural horizon—one in which literature, notably, could no longer claim the preeminence it had traditionally enjoyed—"serious" writers in France scattered, in a variety of directions. Some turned to formal experimentation; others to objectivist techniques; some focused closely upon the banality of daily life; still others began to practice a radical economy of expression.

The minimalists working in France during those years shared a feeling that literature had to pull in its horns if was to remain relevant, that it must dial back its pretensions, take a more modest stand with regard to its purposes, and no longer present itself as a discourse that could totalize human experience. As a cultural gesture, it was probably a useful, invigorating corrective insofar as it defined new terrain and new potential for the novel as a cultural form. One can see it at work on every page of *Narcisse on a Tightrope*, which Targowla conceives in a spirit of most refreshing humility. And even uncertainty, as it were: his sentences are very brief, and their syntax hesitates; he wagers on the fragment as an organizational principle; his narration is curiously circumspect, often eschewing (or deferring) the imperative to *tell*. Granted those features of his style, Targowla puts us to the test as readers, for rather than being passive vessels into which the author pours meaning, we are obliged to *act* here, to exercise our intelligence, our interpretive skill, and our capacity to infer. In short, in the textual contract that Targowla tenders to us, we are invited to accept full franchise in the production of literary meaning. That dynamic, I would like to suggest, is an important component of the way that this novel *performs*.

For, among the many other things it may be, *Narcisse on a Tightrope* is most certainly a performance. As early as the 1960s, the art historian Michael Fried argued that the minimalist impulse is necessarily theatrical in character, since it is so intimately bound up in the actual circumstances in which the beholder encounters the work. It dares us to think about aesthetics in new ways, as it puts on offer a parable of art and its uses. That performance is not without its dangers, moreover, insofar as minimalism takes its stand on the very edges of art, constantly and deliberately flirting with conventional notions of what art is and can be, walking a very fine line between art and non-art. Targowla's novel is no exception: with its deliberately unembellished language, its laconic narrative style, and its apparent impassiveness, it challenges traditional models of prose narrative. At the same time, it invites us to observe and appreciate that process—and to scrutinize our own role therein critically, encouraging us to watch ourselves read, in a sense. In other words, this novel invites us to take our place in this performance, to play our part, and to savor both its perils and its delights.

Once again, earnestly if not particularly subtly, I would like to argue that Targowla's novel and its hero are faced with very similar tasks. For Narcisse's behavior is likewise fundamentally theatrical. He performs for our benefit, a high-wire artist advancing tensively through life, maintaining a very precarious balance as he does so. He is suspended riskily between madness and sanity, inside and outside, self and world, failure and success. And he is working without a net. His funambulism is fascinating. We gaze raptly at him, high above, as he makes his way, slowly, across a chasm of existential threats. Those threats are legion, and they are incarnated in different manners. There are the nurses who seek nothing more than insemination from Narcisse, caring not one whit for who he might be or might become. There are the psychiatrists who see in Narcisse an interesting case study enabling them to advance their careers another notch or two. There are the roommates who come and go, each of whom puts very particular aberrations on display, each playing a different role in the human comedy. There are also the unexamined lumpen, the garden-variety civilians who await Narcisse in the outside world, beyond the hospital's gates, and whom he strains to imagine.

How will he discover his place in that world? How will he find a way to live and abide? Who might he turn out to be? Any readers willing to recognize a dimension of narcissism in their own experience of this text might be tempted to ask a further question: What does all of that mean to *us*? Speaking strictly for myself (as I doubtless ought to do, rather than presuming to know what *you* might think), I watch Narcisse's high-wire act in deep fascination, with bated breath, oblivious to everything around me. While he's up there, inching along, he occupies my spirit entirely, and I can think of nothing else. The notion that he might fall off his tight-rope keeps me on the edge of my seat; yet his balance pleases me, reassures me, and evokes my admiration. Not to put too fine a point on it, his performance plays out the very delights of fiction, a cultural form whose highest expressions likewise can be thought of as tight-rope acts, teetering between this and that, same and other, us and them, rule and anarchy, dread and ecstasy, harmony and dissonance, equilibrium and catastrophe. What more could anyone ask of any performer?

Narcisse on a Tightrope

Chapter 1

ALL OF NARCISSE Dièze's children had nurses for mothers. This was an acknowledged fact: he'd been living at the hospital for seventeen years.

At age forty, he was the presumed father of thirty-five children. This precious piece of information was conveyed to him during a New Year's Eve party when several nurses—with whom he enjoyed fairly close relations—came to lift their glasses and wish him a happy New Year. He wanted to say, "How do you know?" but he didn't dare ask. He put on a knowing expression and blew into his champagne glass.

A nurse called for silence and declared that Narcisse Dièze was actually the father of seventy-two children. She had this from a reliable source, and after all it was a very low figure when you considered the number of nurses who had passed through the hospital, in one unit or another, during the past seventeen years.

Everyone thought about this. A quick mental calculation on that basis could easily support the conclusion that Narcisse was the father of one hundred and seventy-one children. And even that took account only of the nurses who had left the hospital on maternity leave and never returned.

To Narcisse Dièze, the reasons that drove those nurses to get themselves pregnant by him seemed strange, to say the least; but he was so bored by the question that he made no effort to understand.

The first nurse who seduced him had waited less than forty-eight hours to do it. She was young and lithe, and Narcisse, who had just arrived, had found her interest flattering. It wasn't until six months later that he understood the goal of those maneuvers. Exhibiting her rotund stomach with a jubilation he found misplaced, Mademoiselle Dunant had announced that she was sleeping with him solely for the purpose of having a child without being stuck with a partner. His only response had been to gape at her. Naturally, he wasn't taking any precautions and had not inquired about the contraceptive method that Mademoiselle Dunant might be using. That she used some method seemed self-evident, and it would have been unseemly, he felt, to quiz her about such matters.

"But then what will I have to do for the child?"
"You'll never hear a word about it. You already have

more than enough to worry about. And you'll have to spend a certain amount of time here before you can leave. You're pretty sick, after all."

"Isn't there a risk that the child will inherit my illness?"

"Don't worry, I looked into it. Your problem is purely mental and it can't be passed on."

"Ah . . ."

To Narcisse Dièze, Mademoiselle Dunant's way of revealing her true intentions to him had been, to say the least, cavalier.

Anyway, he sulked for several days, but being weak, he gave in again.

Why does she continue to sleep with me, he wondered, since she's gotten what she wanted?

When Mademoiselle Dunant left on maternity leave several weeks later, he knew he would never see her again. He felt a vague regret with regard to the child, but as she had told him, he had his hands full just looking after himself.

The staff noticed that he had long periods of fatigue, during which he slept a lot and ate sparingly, and others during which he was very excited, left his room and paced up and down the corridor.

One morning, as he was stretched out on his bed, wondering whether he felt listless or energized, the nurse who had replaced Mademoiselle Dunant came in. He found her attractive, and he wondered if the little game would start over. He only had to wait until lunchtime for an affirmative answer.

*

Time was passing, nurses came and went. Some would read to him, others would teach him games, still others loaned him books.

Everything considered, Narcisse Dièze found his life agreeable in comparison to other patients' lives—he wasn't suffering in any way—yet unsatisfying in relation to the lives of normal people: he didn't go out, didn't work.

At regular intervals he swallowed impressive quantities of pills, which, according to Doctor Mauméjean, saved him from spending his life in a vegetative state. For that reason, he took them eagerly, and when he had violent stomach pains, he didn't know whether to blame the hospital food or the build-up of medications in his system.

The only moment of suspense in Narcisse's life came during the seventh month of each nurse's pregnancy. He knew that one day soon she would leave without notice—not one had forewarned him in almost seventeen years—and that he would then encounter a new young woman, a new nurse.

Even so, it would be a mistake to suppose that all the nurses in the psychiatric care unit had seduced and then abandoned him.

There were two marked exceptions. Several years before, a new nurse had come into his room. She was very beautiful. Narcisse was so delighted that his heart began racing. But she looked at him as if he weren't there. As a result, he experienced serious doubts about the reality of his own existence.

The situation lasted for six months, during which time Narcisse's mental condition worsened alarmingly. This woman, whom he would never forget, was named Colette Minard. As soon as she opened the door, he would close his eyes. But he couldn't keep them closed for long, for each day he was curious to see how she would lavish various services on him as if he didn't exist. And every day it was heartrending for him to see how adept Colette Minard was at doing what she had to do without anything in her demeanor suggesting that she was attending to a human being.

Things were hardly any better with the next one. But all in all, Dièze still preferred the attitude of this Mademoiselle Dunyach, who approached him with an extreme aversion she didn't try to conceal. He resorted to keeping a mirror on his bedside table to reassure himself after she had left.

Some days Narcisse was convinced she was going to vomit on him, that's how overpowering her disgust seemed to be. And yet—Narcisse had to give the woman her due—not once during the year Mademoiselle Dunyach took care of him did her feelings of revulsion spill out in that most tangible of ways.

*

Throughout his lengthy hospital stay, Narcisse never had occasion to occupy a room of his own. Instead he had a series of more or less congenial roommates, and thus his life was chaotic: he had to keep adapting.

He nonetheless made one friend, Jacazaire, and they had interesting discussions. They talked about their lives before the hospital, their possible futures. As interested as Narcisse was in his own future prospects, Jacazaire was equally passionate about what he'd already done. It must be said that his activities would have taken Narcisse ten lifetimes to accomplish. With some annoyance, the latter couldn't help thinking that Jacazaire's hyperactivity had landed him in the hospital. The attitude of the nurses and doctors was irritating, as well. They spoke to Jacazaire in a respectful tone of voice, which Dièze didn't sense when they spoke to him. And yet, in the two friends' conversations, Jacazaire said nothing to indicate that he saw himself as more import-ant than Narcisse.

Another unsatisfactory aspect of their room-sharing was the positively staggering number of visits that Jacazaire received. He seemed to have a family that Narcisse would never see the end of, even if he lived forever. And Jacazaire's friends were almost as numerous as his family. So, to hide his displeasure at never having any visitors of his own, Dièze took to reading poetry during the afternoon visiting hours. Jacazaire's friends and relatives went to great lengths to draw him into their conversations, but their acts of kindness only irritated him all the more. Narcisse therefore learned to read with such concentration that he would disappear from the world and become totally engrossed in the volume he held in his hands.

Narcisse, who was quite fond of Jacazaire, didn't take offense at these daily invasions, but they left a bitter aftertaste that he usually neutralized with a sip of sugared water.

During their morning discussions, Jacazaire told him that he'd previously done radio broadcasts and given lectures, that he used to teach at the university level, that he'd taken part in meetings of specialists, and that he was developing certain ideas in scholarly journals. He had fallen ill just after signing a contract to write a book that he meant to be definitive, and everyone around him agreed that it would be authoritative, indeed indispensable.

For his part, Dièze had little to say about his past life.

He'd been a bookseller, nothing more. And Jacazaire was tactful enough not to pursue a discussion that would bring a blush to his roommate's face.

*

Jacazaire's morale sustained a serious blow the day the top brass of the hospital—not just those of the psychiatric unit—came to tell him that it was impossible to predict his discharge date. Since the tests were inconclusive, the doctors would have to await the progression of his illness before being able to treat it. That way he could obtain a complete and rapid cure.

"So I'm not sick enough to be cured yet," said Jacazaire, who knew how to boil things down.

"It's more complicated than that," said one of the doctors. "Half the tests we ordered—and we requested the full battery of them—say you are in perfect health, and the other half say you are ill. I'm oversimplifying, of course. Because in fact you've never had all the symptoms of a particular illness, but instead you have some symptoms of every one of a fairly large number of illnesses. Thus, we're treating your symptoms, but alas, with no results for the moment, since from a scientific point of view you don't fall into any diagnostic category. Therefore, you don't have any recognized disorder. It goes without saying that we'll do daily testing until a new finding permits us to identify an illness, which we'll treat, then another, and so forth."

A good fifteen people were present, but the silence that ensued was like that of a deserted sickroom. The doctor who had spoken grew two or three shades paler than Jacazaire. Others had gray faces, while several, in contrast, were crimson. Only four people retained their normal coloring.

Jacazaire looked at the men standing there, and he gave the impression of passing them in review. Several people cleared their throats. Someone even stifled a sneeze.

Then, turning his eyes toward Narcisse, he said to them, "I assume that's everything, gentlemen?" He kept his eyes glued on Narcisse. There was a shuffling of feet, vague mutterings about their next visit, and they were gone.

*

Jacazaire's morale declined gracefully, elegantly. At first Narcisse tried to make conversation but soon realized that he couldn't lift his friend's spirits. Narcisse then became absorbed in reading crime novels. Death was slow in coming. From time to time Jacazaire complained that he would leave nothing of himself but preliminary drafts of his work, to which Dièze replied quite aptly that he himself would leave nothing at all, not even a draft.

"You, at least, can hope."

Narcisse wondered what traces hope could leave, but he didn't want to antagonize his friend.

One Sunday, Dièze fell asleep in the armchair in their room. When he woke up, his book was lying on the floor. He got up. Jacazaire seemed to be sleeping, but he had expired. Narcisse Dièze wept uncontrollably.

Naturally, Narcisse Dièze's sex life slowed down when he had a roommate. His meetings with nurses became furtive, sometimes even impossible. During his time with Jacazaire, Narcisse experienced no carnal desires. The problem, therefore, didn't arise. But he remembered periods when, because he had a roommate, his intimate relationships took on the aspect of an obstacle course. His partners seemed to derive great satisfaction from situations—often awkward and embarrassing—in which the lack of privacy compelled them to squeeze into cramped spaces.

Around the fifteenth year of his hospital stay, Narcisse had a rival. As soon as he saw him enter the room, he knew that things would go badly. Daluzeau was tall and muscular, and he didn't look the least bit ill. Dièze suspected him of treating himself to a vacation courtesy of Social Services. When the neighbor put his suitcase on the bed, they exchanged a long look that portended nothing good. This guy is really obnoxious, Narcisse decided, and he held the intruder's gaze until his eyes stung. Finally looking away with the utmost nonchalance, he reached down to pick up his fallen book and made a show of reading it.

But he wasn't really reading, he was thinking. As physically imposing as Daluzeau was, he was lying in bed just like Narcisse. So there was no reason to develop a complex about him. Besides, Narcisse knew everybody and moved easily in this familiar universe. The newcomer had better behave himself.

Someone knocked on the door. Daluzeau was the first to respond. The new nurse, who was taking a long time to reveal her procreative ambitions in her exchanges with Narcisse, came to inquire if Monsieur Daluzeau had everything he needed. By no means should Monsieur Daluzeau hesitate to ring for her if he needed anything at all, as she didn't have many patients at the moment. Daluzeau turned toward her.

"Call me Michel."
"Oh . . . Of course. I'm Pascaline."

Daluzeau possessed, in addition, a deep, melodious voice. Stupefied, Dièze had seen the self-identified Pascaline blush slightly, which by some strange contagion caused his own face to redden. Noticing the awkwardness of the other two, "Michel" gave a little smile.

For several days a glacial silence prevailed.

The more the doctors showed their indifference to Narcisse, the more Daluzeau became the focus of their attention. He spoke well and had an authority that was understated enough to flatter those he dealt with.

Compared to him, Dièze had the impression that he was diminishing, shrinking. When Doctor Mauméjean asked him routine questions, he would begin by making a gurgling sound and then chortle peculiarly before answering. He would sense his roommate's derision and become increasingly curt in his answers to hide his self-consciousness as much as possible. In any case, Mauméjean didn't waste her time with him. At times he was even beginning to think he had no business being in a hospital.

Pascaline Gavachaud, who was bestowing attention on Narcisse's roommate with an embarrassing insistence, seemed to think that Narcisse needed almost nothing. Out of pride, Narcisse passed two whole days without mentioning that his box of green pills was empty. When she finally noticed, she contented herself with refilling the box without a word of apology. But the worst was still to come.

One day Pascaline Gavachaud came into the room with a folding screen that she set up between the two beds. At first Narcisse was pleased with that. It was a relief not to have to worry anymore about his roommate. But he discovered very quickly that the pretext she

had given for bringing the screen—bathing Daluzeau—
didn't hold up. The predominant sound he heard had
nothing to do with bathing.

A numbness came over him.

With no regard for even minimal decency,
Gavachaud was—beyond any lingering doubt—plea-
suring Daluzeau right there in Narcisse's room. They
spared him nothing. The oral sex went on interminably,
the slurping sounds becoming ever louder and more
explicit. Increasingly abashed—though it seemed that
instead of him it was his two neighbors who should
have felt that way—Dièze noisily shook his newspaper
to remind them that he was still there and that basic
decency should impel them to conduct that type of
activity elsewhere. He even went so far as to force a
cough. But nothing could bring a halt to his neighbors'
frenetic movements on the other side of the screen. A
series of moans punctuated by soft squeals gave him
hope for a moment that their antics were finished.
But that was only the lull before the storm. Narcisse
glanced over from his side of the screen. The rocking
was so intense that he feared for the bed. Then even the
screen began to sway, and at that Narcisse Dièze burst
out laughing, the freest and most resounding laughter
he had ever experienced. Tears were running down his
cheeks. He noted in passing that his neighbors' ardor
was cooling to the point of generating no more than a
murmur.

A few days later, Daluzeau moved out, Gavachaud changed assignments, and Narcisse Dièze took sole possession of the space.

Stretched out on his bed with his hands laid flat at his sides, he felt in harmony with the whole world. Sunlight was streaming into the room, and Narcisse was thinking that his presence there was fitting and right. Anyone viewing Dièze as he was at that precise moment would have thought he was a person humble in spirit who was enjoying a foretaste of heavenly bliss. He was not, alas, such a person, and he was far from blissful. At the very most he was taking advantage of one of those rare moments when he'd attained a certain peace of mind.

Since he found it necessary to adopt some purpose for the day, he spent his time wondering what the new nurse would be like. After Pascaline Gavachaud, he didn't doubt for a second that the next one would be sweet and kind. Maybe even beautiful, he told himself, maybe even beautiful.

The cruel disappointment arrived at the stroke of noon, with the lunchtime meal tray. The nurse was a man. Narcisse had vividly imagined the physical attributes of Pascaline's replacement, but the thought that "she" might be a man had never crossed his mind. A harsh taste permeated his mouth, and he didn't respond to the nurse's banal questions. The man shrugged and left.

Narcisse's anger rose, and he allowed himself a display of moodiness. He showed restraint, however. He settled for hissing a particularly heartfelt insult through his teeth—but only after the departing nurse had shut the door behind him. For Narcisse was always careful not to make enemies if he could help it.

What if the nurse was homosexual? Narcisse never knew how that idea had popped into his head, but suddenly it overshadowed everything else. Very quickly the horror of the situation became apparent to him. He was glued to his bed, at the mercy of this libidinous male nurse, certainly capable of molesting him under a great variety of pretexts. Narcisse was suddenly afraid of the man. Then he wanted to find out whether his fears were well-founded. After all, he told himself, there is nothing to prove that he's homosexual, nor—even if he is—that he wants to assault me.

"Let's be reasonable," he told himself.

But he had to know.

Glancing at the bedside table, he noticed that there

were only two more green pills. He swallowed them in
a brisk gesture and rang for assistance.

He waited. No one came. Trying to calm down,
Narcisse breathed deeply and audibly. After ten minutes, he pressed the button again. Insistently.

Dièze began to think things through. To learn the
truth, he had to be cagey with this nurse, even to
the point of apologizing for his rudeness. Moreover,
Narcisse would have to keep the nurse at a distance,
while at the same time not antagonizing him. People
on the outside have no idea how much patients depend
on their caregivers. If the nurse wanted, he could make
Narcisse's life unbearable. That hadn't often happened
to Narcisse, but he feared it.

The door opened. There had been no knock.
Although not a stickler for niceties, Dièze was wedded
to a certain code of civility, which required every person
to treat others with at least symbolic respect in word or
gesture. But this time, nothing! He wants to come in,
so he pushes the door open. The idea of knocking never
occurs to him. Whether the room is occupied makes no
difference. He enters without knocking, he throws open
the door! A crimson anger spread over Narcisse's face,
a rage boiled up in him: he was capable of anything.

"Did you ring?" A young female nurse, her tone
questioning, was standing in the doorway.

Dièze gulped. This was too much. He buried his face in his hands.

"Are you all right? Do you want me to call the intern?"

She approached him, took his arm, felt his pulse.

"You have a fever. How do you feel?"

You can imagine how hard it was for Narcisse Dièze to reply at such a time. He barely managed a gurgle.

The nurse suddenly looked nervous. She was sure she was dealing with a complication of Dièze's illness. Of course, it was just her luck that this would happen during her first weekend on duty. She mustered a bit of composure when she saw Narcisse calm down and even reach the point of finding the situation comical. He clarified—once he had regained the power of speech—that he just needed some green pills. Reassured, the nurse left.

Dièze wondered when she would come back. If two nurses were caring for him, that could mean only one thing: they were novices.

The young woman returned and cheerfully filled the box with green pills. Narcisse wanted to get acquainted with her.

"You can't have been here long, I've never seen you."

"I started this morning, Monsieur Dièze."

"Monsieur!" He was making an impression on her, then.

"Call me Narcisse," he said, recalling Daluzeau's words.

"I'm going to take your blood pressure, if you don't mind."

She regained some authority as she ran through the accustomed routine. Dièze sighed. At least she had cool hands. He studied her as she performed the procedure. She was a very young nurse. She must have just finished school.

"Is this your first job?"

"You're awfully curious."

"I didn't mean to ask an embarrassing question."

"Not embarrassing, just indiscreet. Yes, it's my first job. One thirty over eighty, not bad." She undid the blood pressure cuff and left before he could continue the conversation.

*

In the following weeks, Dièze had to undergo some tests. They placed electrodes on his body and registered his responses to stimuli on a little monitor that they turned away from him to keep him from seeing the results. Only at the end of the testing did Georges Manzoni, the male nurse, give him the overall results. It took him only three words to do so: good, average, weak. But Narcisse never found out what those words signified in relation to the progression of his illness.

The two nurses took turns coming when Narcisse pressed the call button, and Manzoni came every time there was electrode testing. Despite constant surveillance, Narcisse Dièze was never able to ascertain whether he was homosexual or not.

And it must be said that in time Dièze ceased to be preoccupied with the question.

Chapter 2

On some lonely days, after he'd taken a brown pill, Narcisse let his thoughts drift toward peaceful introspection, like the gentle rocking of a boat on a lake.

He felt so hollow at the core of his being that other people seemed to him to have an exceptional solidity. He reflected rather lackadaisically about his destiny, his identity, his origins.

Nevertheless, these questions did not disturb the serenity of his meditations. The aridity he felt in the depths of himself was perhaps no more than a consequence of his strange illness and one of the reasons for his hospitalization.

But in the final analysis, was he really sick? When he had put the question bluntly to Mauméjean, she'd just shrugged. That had been ages ago, when Dièze was young. On his thirty-fifth birthday he had asked the question again and received this response, almost word-for-word:

"Do you think we're keeping you here for the fun of it? Do you think you would be taking up a bed in a unit as specialized as this if there were another solution? You're being cared for here because you can't be anywhere else. If you were allowed to read your medical records, you'd understand that your question is totally uncalled for."

Narcisse regarded the matter as settled, and his life flowed along in its monotonous, untroubled course. His relationships with the attending nurses were his sole link to the world. He should have been content because he had no concerns of a material nature. And, in fact, he didn't feel unhappy.

Still, he thought, if everyone lived like me, I would probably be quite happy. And yet there are only a handful of people who live this way. All the rest live on the outside. Some well, some badly, but outside and free.

At moments during his mental meanderings, Narcisse Dièze pined for another existence. When he felt that kind of discontent welling up in him, he did what Doctor Mauméjean had told him to do in such cases: he took an orange pill.

After his fortieth birthday, Narcisse spent more time thinking. He had reached the conclusion that he wasn't deriving much enjoyment from life. Everything was happening as if the mere absence of physical suffering was supposed to fulfill and justify his existence.

Without his awareness, however, things around him were changing imperceptibly. The nurses, for example, were sleeping with him less and less, to the point of having no relationship with him beyond a benign indifference. On the other hand, Mauméjean was staying longer to discuss his symptoms.

One day the doctor even delivered a monologue that Narcisse would have liked to record because it was so full of momentous things for him.

Mauméjean had come in the evening without any medical reason: no tests, no medications, no electrodes, no attention to his temperature or other vital signs. She had come in the guise of someone who was paying him a visit. It hardly needs saying that Dièze tensed beneath the covers. Although he was frightened by this new relationship, he very quickly felt a kind of elation.

"Have you noticed that we're now giving you only a few pills per day?"

"Yes, of course, but my daily dosage was reduced several months ago."

"Have you noticed any change in your mental faculties?"

"No. My illness prevents me from making use—full use—of them. I know that well, and you yourself have often explained it to me."

"What I'm about to say will surprise you. In the seventeen years I've known you, I always mistrusted you. I found you dangerous without being able to say exactly why, and to be completely frank I feared that your condition might be contagious. Of course, all that is laughable today and I understand why you find it amusing, but of all the patients on this floor, you were the only one whose harmlessness to others I couldn't vouch for. You'll tell me that the liaisons you had with the attending nurses should have reassured me, but after all, they disappeared in the seventh month of their pregnancies and no one could tell what had become of them. You were a mystery, Dièze. You were a scientific enigma.

"I'm pleased to see that you noticed my use of the past tense. Don't infer too hastily from this that your case has suddenly become clear and that we are in a position to write up a detailed report of your condition, which we have agreed to classify as 'cerebral rheumatism.' But by a phenomenon that science cannot explain, you, Narcisse Dièze, are on the road to a complete recovery. In other words, after a period we deem appropriate, it will be possible for you to leave the hospital and lead a perfectly normal life.

"The look of astonishment on your face tells me it's difficult for you to envision that such a life can lie ahead of you, but it's an idea you'll have to get used to.

"In practical terms, you'll be free to leave your room during a trial period and stroll around the floor. Then we'll give you suitable clothes for going into the other hospital buildings and eventually the grounds. And you'll have to accomplish that by yourself. No one will accompany you. This is Professor Rongemaille's idea. He believes that for you to live independently in the outside world, it's essential for you first to have the opportunity of testing your freedom within our walls.

"We'll get you street clothes—which will be a change from your perennial pajamas—and after that things will be up to you. You'll have sufficient time to readjust, to reintegrate, but no longer than that. Keep that in mind. If you have problems you can't resolve on your own, for the time being you may seek out Madame Colinot, the lead supervisor on the floor. Naturally, you'll be able to come to me if she can't give you the help you need."

Narcisse Dièze had his back against the wall. It would be more accurate to say he was straining against it. Had it been possible, he would have bored his way into it. She was telling him about the end of the world as if it were the most humdrum, ordinary piece of information. He was going to have to do normal things in a normal way, and Mauméjean was announcing this with a smile.

When she got up to leave, he was in a daze, but she seemed not even to notice. For the first time in seventeen years, she touched him, tapping him on the shoulder. "Don't let it bother you, it's easier than it looks. With just a little effort, you'll be like everyone else."

"I'm forty years old!" shouted Dièze.

"That's a wonderful age," she replied.

With a little smile at the corners of her mouth, she turned and left the room.

Once he'd managed to unkink his sore muscles, the first movement he made was to thrust his hand into the box of pills. He put several in his mouth and swallowed them with a glass of water.

Narcisse Dièze wasn't at all sure what he wanted. Dressed in a suit that was slightly too big for him, a roll-neck sweater, and moccasins from another era, he ambled around the hospital corridors. Not knowing where to put his hands, he crossed them behind his back—which helped him think. And in that posture, he quizzed himself about his aspirations.

Before going out into the world, it was crucial for him to know what he did and didn't want. But Narcisse knew nothing at all about the difference between real and false wants. Up to this point, others had done his desiring for him. The nurses had desired him, for example, and he had given in to them. But had he experienced any real desire for them? Is man always a sad creature after coitus, or only when he has mistaken its purpose?

Again and again over a ten-day span, Dièze had left his room dressed in a suit that made him feel uncomfortable, paced the corridors, and marched up and down the stairs. He tried to chat with everyone who seemed willing, but how god-awfully hard it was to start a conversation with someone! He had the impression of having nothing to say, and that made him stumble over his words. Although he had difficulty in speaking, in finding something to say to his fellows, Dièze on the other hand smiled easily. He smiled so much that, without noticing it, he wound up twisting his face into a grimace, as if he were ridiculing the person he was speaking to. He had a very important discussion about this with a male nurse from Senegal.

"The smile," the man told him, "comes at the beginning of the sentence. If you hold it in place too long, either you'll be taken for a fool, or people will think you're treating them like fools."

"But," Narcisse objected, "I just keep smiling because I have no idea what to say to people I don't know."

"It's easy, though. First you smile. Then the other person smiles, it's obligatory. And then you go on to say, 'These corridors are so long I can't find the toilets.' Or, 'Is the library in this building?', when you know it's somewhere else. In either case, the other person feels compelled to stop and talk with you. Once you've gotten the directions, you can move on to how clean the toilets are or what interesting books the library has. Then you ask him if he didn't work in such-and-such a hospital several years ago, because his face looks familiar. From then on, it's a cinch. He'll swap pleasantries with you for a few moments, and the next time you go that way, you'll see him again, and he'll be the one who stops you to chat."

"Yes," replied Narcisse, "it's a good theory. But in practice I feel tongue-tied whenever I have to speak to others. If I start talking a little too soon or a little too late, if my smile is out of sync, I flub my chance, people answer me and walk straight on. Not to mention the times when my voice dies in my throat. Actually, that's what happens most of the time."

"But when you're with me," said the Senegalese nurse, "you speak normally, and your words don't get caught in your throat."

"True, but I know you."

"But you had to get to know me."

"With you it was easy. We passed each other, I smiled and continued on. Just then, you dropped a stack of napkins, and I helped you pick them up. And we laughed together at your clumsiness."

"That's how you get to speak to people, you create a situation. I let go of the napkins."

"On purpose?"

"What do you think?"

"But what if I'd kept going without stopping to help?"

"In that case I would have picked up the napkins. To make new friends, I'm ready for anything. Out of all the people I meet like that, randomly in the corridors, a good half of them become my friends. Life is easier in these big, rambling complexes when you have friends scattered all around."

"Yes, but you're warm, spontaneous, you give the

impression that nothing affects you, that you smile all the time and that you're always happy."

The nurse began to laugh, a deep, husky rumble, practically whispered.

"That's the impression others get, because I don't sulk and I always put on a front. What else should I do, I force myself to look cheerful even when I'm sad or anxious. It's contagious: other people smile back and I end up thinking that I'm happy. Living is a gradually acquired skill, and you have to keep refining it all the time. Otherwise, you rot away in your room like all these phony patients while you wait for the time to go by."

The more time Narcisse spent in street clothes at the hospital, the more uneasy he felt. After two or three days of exhilaration brought on by his change in status, he began to feel jittery, out of place. He failed to see the point of his new life. Up till now he'd been sick, usually stretched out in bed, taking pills at the drop of a hat; thus, there'd been no reason for him to be preoccupied about anything. But these days, wandering the corridors in a borrowed suit, watching for the least sign from another person so that he could make contact, yet at the same time fearing it, Narcisse felt his anxiety building.

He felt oppressed. Luckily, they'd left him two kinds of pills: one he could use in the daytime if he felt uneasy with other people, or when he was too fearful, and the other kind at bedtime to help him fall asleep.

One day, walking the length of the corridor, he noticed a coffee machine. There's the ideal place to meet people, he told himself. He took out a coin and fed it into the machine. The cup dropping into place, the coffee flowing abruptly: all that was somehow commonplace and reassuring.

He picked up his coffee, leaned back against the wall in a relaxed position and waited. Nurses, doctors, visitors passed in front of him. No one looked at him. He even thought that some were deliberately looking away. He shrugged. Either they were avoiding him, or he was just imagining it. Now if he'd been really scary or repulsive, the doctors wouldn't have let him leave his room. Therefore, he was merely imagining that people were shunning him. He went to find a chair in a waiting room and set it next to the machine. He bought another coffee and sat down. A young man came out of a room with a coin in his hand. Without looking at Narcisse, he slipped it into the slot. But Narcisse was not going to miss his chance.

"That machine is handy," he remarked, "and the coffee is good, too."

He made an effort to smile cordially. But the other person, his gaze still evasive, muttered a terse response and went back into his room. Dièze felt his anger rising. The fellow could at least have replied, said something, looked at him directly. Then an obvious fact struck him. The young man was in his pajamas. Therefore, he was a patient. And his illness might involve an aversion to engaging with others. "Even so . . ." Narcisse had groaned.

It's a start, mused Narcisse as he stood up. He tossed his cup into a wastebasket, set his chair back in its place, and continued his walk, with a sense of tolerance toward others that did him good.

The telephone started ringing. Narcisse was alone in his room. He let it ring several times, hoping that whoever was calling would hang up. He had just returned from walking the corridors and hadn't yet taken off his suit jacket.

What persuaded him to pick up the phone was his certainty that it was a wrong number. No one ever called him.

"Narcisse Dièze. It's Maumejean."
He didn't speak.
"Are you there, Monsieur Dièze?"
"Yes."
"Ah, there you are. I have news for you. I would like you to meet someone you'll be dealing with after your discharge. Could you come to my office tomorrow afternoon around three?"
"Yes."
"Don't be nervous, Narcisse. It has to do with explaining what's going to happen for you next week and making sure you understand. I think you'll find it interesting. And the person you're going to meet is very

nice. I won't say anymore, we'll sort this out face-to-face. See you tomorrow, Monsieur Dièze."

When Narcisse put down the phone, he was deluged with conflicting emotions. Fear, certainly. Who was this person they were going to have him meet, and exactly what did they expect of him? Excitement, too. Mauméjean's tone was entirely new. She'd spoken to him the way people did out in the world when they were setting up appointments. She hadn't really given him any choice as to the date and time, but could he have credibly said that he was sorry, he had another engagement the next day, right at three o'clock?

He went to the window and looked outside. The afternoon was lovely and the sun hadn't set. For the first time in a long while, Narcisse opened the window. He heard the thrum of distant traffic, the echo of footsteps. The scent of freshly mown grass drifted up to him. For no reason, he had tears in his eyes. He called himself an imbecile and sat down in the stuffed armchair to await the arrival of his dinner.

His life was about to change. They were going to tell him he had to leave now and stop going in circles within the hospital. But Narcisse wasn't ready to confront an exterior world he knew nothing about. He might be a danger to other people, what did they know of that? And furthermore, why leave? He was doing well here. In any case he was quite used to it. He'd forgotten everything about the outside. He'd never manage it.

Nonetheless, he reflected, I'd like to lead a normal existence, to work like other people, to feel what they do, to spend my daily life with them, not just stay under this glass dome that's slowly smothering me. But is it really possible to return to the world after a seventeen-year absence? Mauméjean said I was cured. Easy for her to say! Whether I'm cured or not, she isn't the one who'll have to run up against all the problems of living out there. If they were still giving me special medications, those might help me adapt. But do such things exist? Has anyone thought to make pills that comfort frightened people? There must be some sedative that makes it bearable to live in society. That's a question I'll have to bring up tomorrow. Even if it's the only one I dare to bring up, I'll need to get a straight answer.

There was a knock at the door. A young woman set a tray on the table and wished him an enjoyable meal. Narcisse stood up, fetched a chair and sat down at the table.

Keeping his eyes closed, Narcisse tried to prolong his night's sleep. Knowing that a difficult day awaited him, he wanted to get up as late as possible. He considered taking a sleeping pill. But the day had surely dawned, and if he took a sleeping pill now, he'd sleep too long and be in poor shape for his meeting. On the other hand, if he took one of his daytime pills, it wouldn't make him drowsy. So Narcisse decided to open his eyes. He looked at his watch and saw with satisfaction that it was already eight a.m. Therefore, he had slept longer than usual. He got up, gathered his toiletries and went to the communal bathroom. Dièze felt good, and he took a long, scalding shower. He washed his hair and shaved meticulously. He had to summon up all his resources.

When he returned to his room, the breakfast tray was there. He poured a full cup of coffee and grimaced as he forced it down without sugar: he needed to get himself going.

Around ten o'clock he entered the web of corridors, descended several levels and climbed back up to

another. A quarter of an hour later, he was in the corridor where Mauméjean's office was located. There was
a window at the end and the sun was illuminating the
passage. Narcisse noted the sun's presence as an excellent omen and mused that at three o'clock it would
no longer be there. But he had scouted out the meeting place and the situation looked promising. He went
away humming to himself.

Smoking a filter cigarette in his room, Narcisse waited
for the meeting time. He was sitting in his red, imita-
tion-leather armchair near the open window, astonished
at what he could only call a sense of inner well-being.
Though he had every reason in the world to worry, he
felt relaxed and in tune with himself. Never before had
he experienced such an absence of anxiety, and he wondered if that could be evidence of his recovery. But he
immediately reconsidered. Surely it was just a passing
state of mind. He glanced up at the wall clock and rose
abruptly from the chair. Unthinkingly, he flicked his
cigarette butt out the window. Then he hurriedly looked
to see whether anyone below had been harmed by his
impulsive gesture. Reassured on that score, he slipped
on his pants, donned his jacket, cleared his throat and
dashed out of the room.

   Doctor Mauméjean's office door seemed more imposing than when he'd sized it up earlier, but since it was
too late to slink away, he knocked. The response came
as he was knocking a second time, and he opened the
door with some embarrassment. Maybe he'd knocked
too insistently.

Mauméjean was waiting for him, standing behind her desk. Narcisse remarked with surprise that he was taller than she was. Before sitting down in the chair she offered him, he had time to notice that she seemed distracted.

"Are you still determined to leave the hospital?"

"Yes . . . or rather, no. I mean, isn't that what's been said?"

"My question for you," said the doctor as she walked back and forth behind her desk, "is whether you really want to leave here and confront the outside world. Because if you lack the will to do this, Narcisse, you have no chance. Your condition could get worse if this experience isn't driven by a keen desire."

A migraine was settling in behind Narcisse's forehead. His eyesight grew clouded, and he became aware of a buzzing sensation in his ears. A single sentence resonated in his skull: "What is all this rigmarole?"

Mauméjean, however, sat down at her desk. She seemed a little calmer.

"You need to understand, Narcisse. Your discharge is not an easy thing. I feel somewhat responsible for you. I look at you sitting there in front of me and I think, 'What will he do if he suffers an acute episode? Is he capable of dealing with the problems that are going to arise?' From what we currently know about your disease, your recovery depends entirely on your inner confidence. We reduced your medications, and then we even substituted natural, gently acting remedies. And the symptoms of your illness were disappearing one after another. We've drawn no conclusions about your apparent cure except that something in you appeared to heal you organically, probably without your knowledge. So all that is well and good, but you really must reflect and tell me, yes or no, whether you are all but certain you'll be able to cope.

"Do you understand, Narcisse?"

Not only did Narcisse fail to understand, but a rage was seething inside him, and he couldn't keep it contained. He looked out the window, took a deep breath. Nothing worked. He felt himself turning purple. His fury took hold and he had to speak, had to vent, or else he would die on the spot, choked by his own anger.

The explosion took place. It lasted only a few minutes, but to Narcisse it seemed interminable. He heard himself saying horrible things. Insulting Mauméjean. The hospital, the nurses, all those who had—in his words—made him physically ill. And now that he was in a position to leave, he was being forced to give her still more assurances. Wasn't it hard enough without them piling on even more difficulties? "'All but certain'! Why not ask for an engraved warranty while you're at it?"

Dièze stopped abruptly. He might as well have been barking at the moon.

Numbed, stupefied, terrified by his inability to control such a violent outburst, Narcisse held his breath, his eyes lowered.

"Now then, Monsieur Dièze, we've just heard something that contrasts strikingly with what I've observed of your character during these seventeen years! What's gotten into mild, timid Monsieur Dièze?"

Narcisse gulped. He glanced at the doctor: she looked delighted. He wanted to apologize, but he realized it wouldn't be appropriate. That was not what was expected of him. And to be perfectly frank, he felt good, relieved to have thrown a tantrum. Little by little, to his own satisfaction, he felt himself becoming giddy, as if under the effect of a drug.

Mauméjean and Narcisse looked at each other and broke out laughing at the same instant. Helpless, uproarious laughter. He had the feeling that tightly coiled springs were loosening inside him.

*

The doctor went out for coffee. When she returned, she handed a cup to Narcisse, and they toasted each other with their plastic cups.

"Now we must definitely collect our wits," she said. She looked at her watch.

"I asked Professor Perrolaz to join us after you and I had spoken by ourselves. He'll be here shortly."

"Oh! It's fine for him to come right now," said Narcisse, swallowing the last of his coffee.

*

Perrolaz was an affable man who seemed very glad to find Narcisse there, even though he had never seen him before. He had a beaming smile and Narcisse fell instantly under his spell. After exchanging a few words with Mauméjean, he sat down on the easy chair near Narcisse and set his briefcase on the floor. It was an attaché case stuffed to the bursting point; the zipper had been broken for ages.

"So, Monsieur Dièze, where do you stand on all this?"

Perrolaz seemed to rejoice in advance at the good news that Narcisse was sure to give him. Dièze, rather intimidated by a joviality beyond anything he'd ever encountered, risked a few sentences in an unsteady voice.

"Well, I believe I'm going to be able to leave. Or at the very least try. I feel better."

"Now that's a good attitude! You must believe in it, Monsieur Dièze, it's a precondition to your success. I mean to say, to your recovery."

Perrolaz glanced at Mauméjean, who was listening to him with her hands folded on her desk. Turning back toward Narcisse, his face became soberer, more serious—more normal, in a way.

"Your own prognosis is good, but I think you should know what is happening with the other patients who are on the way to being cured. Up to now, we've recorded seventeen cases of cerebral rheumatism involving patients who, like you, have progressed toward recovery. Of these seventeen patients, thirteen have had the experience of living outside the hospital. The other four lost their nerve before their planned discharge. What can I say? Right on the verge of leaving. Of the thirteen patients who have lived on the outside, eight are considered today to be definitively cured. Five couldn't tolerate the experience and returned to the hospital as inpatients, where their condition is stable. I tell you this to indicate that you are not taking a big risk. At worst you return to your previous situation and at best you live a normal life. Surely that's worth a try, isn't it?"

When the professor paused, Narcisse wondered how to respond. He ran through sentences in his head. In vain, for none of them fit the situation. He therefore preferred to let a silence prevail among the professor, the doctor and himself. It was Maumérjean who intervened at last.

"Perhaps it's risky to say this now, but considering the eight cases we've had occasion to study, it seems to me that Monsieur Dièze represents the type of patient who is destined to be cured. From what we know of him, he presents all the positive aspects encountered in the other cases, but never before in a single person. In other words, Monsieur Dièze, you are our model patient," she added as she turned to face him.

"Ah . . ."

"Don't let that disturb you," added Perrolaz. "In our opinion, it gives you better odds than any of the eight people who are now completely cured. From our perspective, there's hardly any chance that you won't be completely cured."

Narcisse gradually regained a measure of confidence.
"You're saying that just to encourage me. You must have said the same thing to the other seventeen."
He had spoken in a soft voice, but he felt composed enough to be taken seriously. Seated squarely in his chair, he waited for their response. There was even, it seemed, a mischievous gleam in his eyes.

Perrolaz and Mauméjean replied simultaneously, and this is more or less what they said:
P.—"We said nothing to the others, and . . ."
M.—"We aren't trying to trick you . . ."

Everyone laughed discreetly, and Perrolaz was the first to resume.
"Don't think that. We had behavioral records for each person. Very detailed records, and it was in comparing

them with yours that we discovered that you were the composite of our other patients. In any case, it's you and you alone who can confirm or negate our prognosis. Beginning tomorrow, you will hold your destiny in your own hands. It will be up to you."

Narcisse cleared his throat and asked the question he'd promised himself he would raise.

"Are there pills to help me cope in case of difficulties on the outside? Or with other people?"

"Absolutely!"

Perrolaz's voice became warmer, more expansive.

"Absolutely. We'll give you two kinds of pills, one for difficulties you might encounter during the day, and the other in case you suffer from insomnia. Besides, don't forget that you'll be spending your nights at the hospital, and I'll be available if you need anything at all. By the way, I don't think you know where my office is located. Would you like me to show you the way? It's best that you know how to find it if you need to talk to me after your days of freedom. Doctor Maumèjean, would you excuse us?"

Maumèjean's answering smile conveyed enough for Narcisse to recognize that this was a rehearsed skit. But he was feeling indulgent, and the idea of meeting separately with Perrolaz was far from displeasing to him.

*

They walked the corridors in silence, went down the

stairs and passed through the grounds to another building. Dièze noted that it housed both the professor's
office and his own room, the latter one floor higher.

Perrolaz opened a door and beckoned his patient
to enter. As he did so, Narcisse had the impression of
a very strong intimacy with the professor. That both
pleased and troubled him. The spacious room was
furnished with an antique desk, modern chairs, and
a bookcase bulging with volumes. Narcisse surprised
himself by sitting down without being asked.

"Would you like something to drink?"
The question caught Narcisse off guard, and he
couldn't reply. It didn't jibe with the exchanges he was
used to.
"Don't be afraid, I'm not trying to get you tipsy. It's
just that we have to talk about important things, and I
don't think a glass of port would be out of order under
the circumstances. Unless you don't like that idea?"
"Oh, but I do," said Narcisse, though he was feeling
more and more uncomfortable.
"That's splendid," said Perrolaz, opening a cabinet
from which he withdrew an oddly shaped bottle and two
small glasses. He set everything on the desk. Filled the
glasses. The port had an inviting hue. He put a glass in
Narcisse's hand, took the other and sat down at his desk.
"To your health, Dièze, in every sense of the word,"
he said, lifting his glass.
Narcisse raised his glass and muttered something

about the different senses of the word not being very clear to him.

"Physical health, mental health!" said Perrolaz. "We're all in the same boat, you know, and it's also what I wish for myself."

He chuckled with a touch of bitterness.

Then he returned to being both genial and earnest.

"Narcisse," he said, "you'll surely need to talk about the experiences you have on the outside. There will undoubtedly be some things you don't understand, others that will frighten you, still others that will give you pleasure. I think it would be desirable for you to return every evening about six o'clock and come by for a talk with either Mauméjean or me. What do you think about that?"

"I . . . yes, certainly," said Narcisse as he drank a large gulp.

"Relax, Narcisse, and answer me."

"Well, I don't know. Yes, it's certainly good to talk every evening. But I don't know whether I'll have any-thing to say. You know I have no idea what's in store for me on the outside, so for me to tell you whether I'll need to talk . . ."

"True enough. But I'm only making an offer. If you don't feel like talking, don't come, that's all. I won't hold it against you. I just want you to know that my door will always be open to you."

"Very well," said Narcisse. "I'm taking special note of that."

His words made him smile.

Perrolaz stood up. He seemed ill at ease. He drained his drink, set his glass on the desk and began pacing back and forth. He was unable to stand still. Narcisse emptied his glass, crossed his legs and looked at Perrolaz with a certain satisfaction. Was this an effect of the alcohol? He felt he was the professor's equal. To feel like someone's equal, and not like an inferior or an invalid, had something intoxicating about it.

After striding to and fro for a while, Perrolaz finished by setting his elbows on the piece of furniture that served as his bar and said, "I owe you the whole truth. You'll need to discuss your experiences on the outside, but I also need to hear about them. You see, I'm one of the few specialists in cerebral rheumatism, and for many years I've been writing a book on the subject. The purely medical part is done, but what I lack is the experience of a recovering patient who has left the hospital. I know you'll say that the eight fully recovered patients must have spoken to me. Well, believe it or not, they couldn't tell me much of anything. Oh, they described their sensations, their emotions, but in such a cursory way that I was unable to use the information for my book. Now you can well imagine that a book on cerebral rheumatism would be woefully incomplete if it failed to describe the progression of the recovering patient on his way to reconnecting with society. So I'm asking you, Monsieur Dièze, to make an effort, from the time of your discharge, to remember the events that you experience so that you can tell me about them in as precise a manner as possible. I'm asking you this as a favor."

Right then, Narcisse could have told the professor that he was experiencing a moment of mild euphoria. That he felt normal in a way he'd never felt before. But he had no wish to spoil this sensation by talking about it. He contented himself with nodding.

"On top of that," continued Perrolaz, "you're our model patient, as the doctor told you a little while ago. Thus, we'll be able to generalize from your experience to that of the other cured patients, the ones who haven't been able to describe it to me. In any case, I don't need your answer right now. I simply wanted you to know that your experience and your discharge tomorrow far transcend your personal case. Naturally, though, if you can't recount your experiences any better than the others, well, we'll adjust to the situation."

The professor paused for a moment and continued while gazing at Narcisse with an engaging smile.

"At least we will have tried everything."

In his room on the seventh floor of a building at the southern edge of the hospital campus, Narcisse Dièze felt a sense of confinement. Stretched out on his bed with his hands behind his head, he was staring at the ceiling and daydreaming. He visualized himself in the escape chamber of a submarine, ready to rise toward the surface. Then he imagined all the dangers that were awaiting him, and each time he retreated to the main compartment. In the end, he felt oppressed. It was the last Sunday before his discharge, the weather was lovely, and yet he hadn't the least interest in going out for a walk. A chill penetrated his chest. He got up and edged around the bed. His new room was quite cramped. Narcisse took comfort in telling himself that he would be there only in the evening and that his living quarters were therefore of little importance. Feeling colder and colder, he put on his raincoat over his suit jacket. But nothing helped, the cold was still getting the better of him, and Dièze had the feeling that the warm air he was inhaling had turned ice cold by the time it reached his lungs.

He decided to go out. Then hesitated. Said in a

hushed voice that he was afraid of catching cold. The truth, he added silently, is that I'm afraid to go out. Reluctantly, he descended the stairs, his raincoat buttoned to the neck. When he reached the bottom, he tried to push open the door to the hospital grounds, when he should have pulled it. Though he saw a bad omen in that, he had no wish to go back upstairs. Since he had to go out, that's what he'd do. He pulled the door open and found himself outside. His whole body began to shiver. The muscles in his back tightened. Narcisse didn't like the outside air. He took first one step, then another. He set off at a slow, shuffling pace. His body more and more chilled, Narcisse felt infirm. Could the weather be this cold in June? He looked around. Lightly dressed patients and visitors were walking nearby. Thus, it was he who was producing the cold. It was in him. Little by little he felt the sun's warmth on his face and within his body, beneath his raincoat. Narcisse experienced conflicting sensations. The cold was dammed up inside him. His teeth were chattering. But he would not have returned to his room for anything in the world. He had to carry on. Feeling weary, he searched out a bench in direct sunlight and sank onto it. The warmth pouring down on him and the cold embedded within were waging a strange combat. He felt like a puppet being jerked in two directions.

Racked by spasms, Narcisse wondered if he was dying.

The sun made Dièze sweat profusely. He was

overheated. He opened his raincoat and forced himself to breathe slowly. Moments later the sensation of inner cold receded. Narcisse was trembling less. He took off his raincoat, then his suit jacket. He even unbuttoned his shirt. It was drenched with perspiration. He ran his hand over his forehead; it, too, was wet. A gentle breeze came up and Narcisse resumed walking. He sought out the shade of the trees and continued his stroll until he felt almost dry. The scent of the undergrowth, the shouts of children, the blare of a radio—all those reached him simultaneously, and he felt he had won a furious battle. He returned to his room, undressed and took a shower. He changed his clothes and went out again.

This time his excursion was a pleasant one. "A beautiful summer day," an old gentleman told him. Narcisse smiled at him and nodded. Words still didn't pass his lips. He saw a man in pajamas who was walking with assistance from a young woman. Dièze approached them to see if they were wearing wedding rings. They were, in fact, and for no particular reason that made him happy.

"Tomorrow at this time, I'll be on the outside," he thought. "It had to happen sometime." Narcisse let out a resentful little laugh.

Chapter 3

HE WAS STALLED in the middle of the sidewalk, unable to move either forward or backward. He held his breath. He was lightly jostled—a man stepping aside to avoid him accidentally brushed him with his shoulder—and then a child got tangled up in his legs. A kind of rolling wave was building up inside him, and he recognized it as panic. As if reaching him from above, a medley of guidance entered his mind. "Put on a show of bravado," "take a deep breath," "keep your fear out of sight." Mustering a mighty effort, he managed to pivot to his right and pretend to be looking at a shop window. But he had to take a step closer. He let out a deep sigh, thrust out his right leg, moved forward, and bumped into the windowpane. Hoping no one had noticed, he stood stock-still as he tried to focus his gaze on the objects on display. Passersby still nudged him at times, for the sidewalk was not wide, but more often they stepped off the curb to avoid him.

Narcisse Dièze began to reconstruct in his mind the things that had been happening to him. His muscles were locked, his breathing barely sufficient. A sensation of frost and chill was growing in him. What should he do?

At first, his departure from the hospital had gone well. Before setting out, he'd spent an hour walking within the hospital grounds, making a point of greeting everyone he encountered. He had received a response every time, and he soon felt confident enough to venture into the street, suitcase in hand. He'd feared this particular moment, the instant when he would pass through the hospital's covered entryway and find himself in the open. A succession of steps—he refrained from directing them too consciously—did the trick for him.

Once outside, he was surprised not to feel a great sense of elation. No, he was outside, he was content, that was the extent of it. He began walking aimlessly, and he didn't need a destination to experience the pleasure of walking. He was walking almost like everyone else. To be sure, the others were going much faster, but they were swept along by a purpose, they were headed somewhere. The constant stream of movement was alarming, clamorous, threatening, unnerving, but Narcisse was not troubled by it. The external world did not yet terrify him. His interior world was still keeping him busy. At an intersection he looked up and read

the name of the road he was following: Boulevard de
l'Hôpital. That seemed like a good omen to him, and he
continued his slow course. Pedestrians passed on his left
and right without noticing him. He decided to move
closer to the shops, and once he'd done so, others could
pass him only on his left. That was an improvement.
He gave a little smile. But soon afterward, without the
slightest warning, a paralysis came over him on a side
street. That was how Narcisse Dièze had come face-to-
face with his own reflection, completely immobilized,
struggling to control the panic that was mounting in
him.

The first thing he managed to do was moderate
his breathing. While he pretended to be particularly
absorbed by the baubles in the shop window, he was
trying to move his feet and activate his arms. It took
him fifteen minutes to regain the use of his limbs. Yet
his anxiety had not eased. He needed a pill right away.
He had some in his pocket, but he couldn't swallow one
without water. Therefore, he had to—he'd have to—
find a café. Cautiously turning his head to his right,
he could see nothing of that nature. On his left, again
nothing. His problem had no solution. He looked
through his reflection at the inside of the shop. He saw
piles of small objects that appeared to be souvenirs from
more or less everywhere. A young woman was watching
him from the back of the shop. At first, he was shocked
to be seen in such an embarrassing situation. But that
person could help him meet his most pressing need, a

glass of water. Stiffly, carefully, he made his way to the shop entrance.

Very soon after crossing the threshold, he sensed he'd be dealing with a friendly person. Already the young woman was moving toward him and making eye contact. She asked him what he wanted. And suddenly, his mind was completely muddled. A swarm of words buzzed around in his head, to the point that nothing could emerge. When the young woman posed the question again in different terms, he was finally able to retrieve the necessary question from his panicked state: "Could you . . . a glass of water?"

Relieved to have summoned the words, he let out a sigh. The young woman seemed uneasy, no doubt wondering if she was dealing with a madman. But she must have decided there was nothing to fear, since she invited him to sit down—which he gratefully did, as his rigid muscles had exhausted him.

He began again: "Would it be possible to have a glass of water? I need to take a pill."

The shop assistant hesitated no longer and disappeared into the back room.

A mellow warmth was coming over Narcisse. Certainly, the sensation of an inner chill remained, squeezing his chest, but being able to express himself, to ask for something and obtain it, was giving him a pleasing sense of reconnecting with society.

She returned with a glass of water. Narcisse took the glass, thanked her, and began searching his pockets for his pillbox. A few drops of water spilled on him, and the shop assistant relieved him of the glass. Rummaging through his pockets, he extracted the little container, opened it, and took out a white pill. She handed back the glass, he took a sip with the pill, and that was that. Even before the medicine had time to take effect, Narcisse was already feeling better. Almost good.

"Are you ill?"

"No," he replied. "On the contrary. But I just got out of the hospital, and I'm kind of weak."

"You're very pale. Would you like me to call the hospital?"

All at once, everything was jumbled in Narcisse's head. Why would she want him to go back to the place he'd just left?

"No, certainly not. Hold on, I'll show you my discharge letter."

"No, no, I believe you. There's no need."

Narcisse, in his eagerness to justify himself, spilled the rest of his water on his pants and on the shop's carpet. The young woman retrieved the empty glass from his hands and told him the water wouldn't stain the carpet, that it didn't matter. He nonetheless fished out his wallet—very thin—and removed the precious letter. She shook her head and said that if he was feeling better, he should leave. That was the logical thing to do. He straightened up, took hold of his suitcase, and left the store, remembering to thank the shop assistant.

Back outside, he resumed his slow amble. His anxiety seemed under control, but his steps began to falter, and he realized that the way he was headed didn't suit him. He made an about-face.

He couldn't have said how long he'd gone on walking—surely for quite a while. More than once, he'd even circled blocks of houses repeatedly. Navigating the streets demanded efforts that seemed beyond him. Thus it was that he fetched up by chance in front of a brasserie. And there, without hesitation, as if he'd been doing it all his life, he pushed open the door and strode resolutely inside. Predictably, his way was briefly obstructed by men huddled at the bar who were telling stories in which sweeping hand gestures seemed to be an essential element. And of course, they made no apologies; no doubt they hadn't even noticed. He nonetheless pressed on into the back room, with the distinct intention of sitting there. He found a table near the bay window and sat down at it. From that vantage he could survey the street without getting jostled. His idea had been a good one. He looked around contentedly.

He would have liked to call over the waiter to take his order, but he didn't dare. He waited politely at the table, his suitcase at his feet, his hands folded on his knees, his eyes staring into space. Besides, he didn't know what he wanted. Was he hungry? Thirsty? During his hospital stay, his wants had been defined by others. Everything would have to be relearned. Therefore, he ordered the first thing that came into his mind: a small glass of beer. The waiter asked him to be more specific, listing all the brands of beer on offer in the establishment. Narcisse chose a brand name that seemed to have a nice ring to it.

Once again, he was tensing up. It was getting hard to move his limbs, and his brain couldn't control the degree of panic that was surging inside him. He took out his box of pills and set it on the table. He looked outside. No one on the street was showing signs of anxiety. All the pedestrians were obeying a normal logic of movement, and their faces betrayed minds that had no room for doubt. Whether they were children, adolescents, adults, men, women, no one lacked confidence, and that terrified him. The waiter served him his beer. A lovely ray of sunlight pierced it. Narcisse was grateful to the waiter, even though it was clear that chance alone deserved the gratitude.

At first, Dièze tried hard to keep each passerby in sight as long as possible, aiming to solve the mystery of the difference between him and them. He followed them one by one, and then by small groups. He held them in his imagination even after they'd disappeared. He scanned the cars, the trucks, observing their drivers stopped at the red light. With time, he developed the feeling of understanding others better. He didn't quite know what he'd understood, but it seemed to be something fundamental.

After that, he concentrated on his beer.

Everyone drank it in all the countries of the world,
and Narcisse had not drunk any for seventeen years. He
was dreading the first swallow. He had reconnected with
the noise, the smells, the bustle, and the physical con-
tacts of the exterior world, but the experience of tasting
was still to come. He was afraid he'd be disappointed.
He took the glass in his hand and raised it to his nose.
The smell was unremarkable. After once again holding
up the beer in the sunlight, he took a sip.

Stunning! He remembered this taste, but the passing years had greatly attenuated it in his memory. This
time, he felt the taste directly on his tongue, and the
fermented liquid stimulated his palate. The beer was
Narcisse Dièze's first pleasure in the outside world.

Little by little, his brain yielded to tipsiness. He was
gazing at the empty glass sitting next to his pillbox on
the little round table. In his mildly euphoric state, he
felt very much as though he belonged there.

"Would you like to order lunch?"

It seemed to take forever for Narcisse to turn toward
the waiter. The latter, repressing a momentary irritation,
repeated his question.

"Yes, indeed. Why not?"

"I'll bring you the menu."

It is hard to describe the state in which our character
found himself. Precarious in the world, and yet capable
of commanding respect because he had a sense of what

to say and do. The exhilarating effect of the beer gave him the feeling of occupying a space that was neither the hospital nor the outside world. As if on a tightrope.

When he opened the fold-out menu, the words quickly blurred before his eyes. There were so many choices that nothing was real anymore. Even when he concentrated on an item, Dièze was unable to fathom the dish it was describing. He didn't want to ask for explanations, fearing he wouldn't understand them any better. He went with steak frites and a large glass of red wine. His chosen dish had the advantage in his eyes of being one that wasn't available at the hospital and not too far afield from his cultural references.

He stretched out his legs against the lower edge of the bay window. People were beginning to enter the brasserie as if they were being pursued. The weather was lovely, however, and the balmy temperature was more conducive to strolling than to haste. Even so, the people outside were in the latter mode: they were practically running. An attractive woman had just sat down at a table near his. He smiled blissfully at her, but she failed to smile in return. No doubt she needed a beer, too. Then two men, manifestly regular customers, came to sit in a corner behind Narcisse and began to converse loudly and howl at each other's jokes. Their banter grated terribly on his ears, and he preferred to stare at his neighbor's legs. But someone outside caught his attention as she approached the front door. The young shop assistant recognized him, too, which made her visibly hesitant to enter the premises, where she was undoubtedly a regular like the others.

Dièze smiled at her, and she returned a truncated little smile. She started forward again and entered the brasserie. She came up to him and asked about his health. He invited her to join him at the table, but she swiftly declined.

"No. I thank you for the invitation, but I'm having lunch at the bar." Narcisse lowered his head in disappointment and wished her a pleasant meal after she had already moved on.

*

The steak was hard to chew. He was no longer accustomed to chewy foods. His jaws might have lost some strength during his hospital years. He was even afraid of breaking his teeth. But by concentrating on chewing, he managed to eat. It turned out that the meat wasn't so tough, after all. And the frites were crunchy. "Like when I was a little boy," thought Narcisse, which astounded him, for in normal times he never thought of his childhood. It's true that he had departed that morning from what had long been "normal times." More precisely, departed from his own normal time to enter other people's. All that gave him a headache. The wine didn't surprise him. He'd drunk some of it at the hospital. But its taste went well with the food. After a little rush of distress due to the difficulty he had with chewing, Dièze returned to the state of delight induced by his discovery of the real world. He ordered a strong espresso to accentuate the difference between it and the weaker version dispensed in disposable cups during his hospital days. They served him an ounce or so in a little china cup. He sank a cube of sugar in it. He used his spoon to dissolve the sugar. He stirred for a long time to assure a perfect blend. He gulped down the coffee and burned his mouth. But the taste was there. Strong and bitter.

As he left the brasserie, Narcisse Dièze looked at his watch. It was two in the afternoon, and he was free until seven. He was determined not to waste a minute of his newfound freedom. And yet, plodding slowly along, suitcase in hand, he didn't see how he could occupy the time. He would have liked to leave his suitcase somewhere: though it wasn't heavy, it was embarrassing. He thought of storing it in a train station locker, but there was no station nearby. So, he walked, or rather dawdled along, until his steps led him to the shop where the young woman worked. He looked through the shop window and saw her at the back of the shop, looking very cute. He pushed open the door.

"Hello again. I'm not disturbing you, am I?"

"That depends. What do you want?"

"Well, to ask a favor of you. I have an appointment at seven this evening, and I'd like to go walking from now till then without having to carry my suitcase. If it wouldn't trouble you, I'd really like to leave it in a corner here. Unless that would bother you."

"Listen, I don't know you, I don't know what's in that suitcase. I'd rather you find another solution."

Dièze was astonished. He didn't see how the contents

of the suitcase could make the young woman uneasy.
But he made a point of opening it in front of her.

"You see, it's just the usual. Some fresh clothes, toiletries. What did you think I was carrying?"

"You never know. OK, you can leave it here. But if
you don't come back before the store closes, I'll put it
on the sidewalk. I'm just a sales assistant here."

Narcisse realized that his problem was solved, and
he felt even freer as he was leaving. He strolled along
with his hands in his pockets. The air was mild. He was
borne along by good spirits now and felt more at ease
in the city.

Never had his mind been less cluttered. He was merely a body in motion. He eyed the other pedestrians. By and large, no one was really paying attention to him. He wasn't offended by that: they were living a routine day, he an extraordinary one. He found himself in a square. There were unoccupied benches, and he sat down at one for a rest. His legs outstretched, his arms crossed, Dièze was watching the children playing in a sandbox. Then he looked at their mothers. One of them abruptly turned her head away. Surprised, Narcisse tried to make out her face, but she had retreated behind her neighbor, a woman of a certain plumpness. Narcisse turned his gaze back to the sandbox. Two boys were arguing over the possession of a toy rake. Other children were observing the dispute, sitting or standing near the adversaries, and the mothers were also attentively viewing the scene, notably, one would imagine, the mothers of the children involved. The dispute was like all childhood squabbles. But something intrigued Narcisse. The smaller of the two boys remained silent, while his opponent was yelling. The smaller boy suddenly let go of the rake. Caught unaware, the other boy lurched several steps backwards. He lost his balance, then recovered it and looked at his rival with a triumphant glare spread across his face. The smaller boy rushed forward and thrust his fist into the opponent's face, exactly as an adult or adolescent would have done. A right hook to the chops. The little assailant must have been about three. The victim dropped the rake and dashed toward his mother, who took off in his direction while trying to meet the eyes of the offending child's mother. The latter came forward to reproach her son for the violent blow he had dealt his little comrade, who was bleeding slightly.

There was quite an uproar, and it was not uninteresting to watch. It took a good fifteen minutes for the mothers to calm down. Then the perpetrator and his mother decided to leave, pursued by the hateful glares of the group that had taken the victim's side. Narcisse heard remarks like "the little brat," "if that's how she's raising him, there'll be hell to pay," and other equally genteel comments. The aggressor and his mother went past Narcisse, who gave them a supportive little wave. He had quite liked the youngster's punch. The woman's face was beet red. She looked straight ahead. And he recognized her.

"Mademoiselle Faure!"

Clearly, he should have said "Madame," but the other expression had come to him spontaneously.

"Ah, Monsieur Dièze!"

She had no intention of stopping. Holding her child's hand, she was scampering off. Narcisse caught up with her.

"Aren't you surprised to see me out of the hospital?"

"Yes, I am. But excuse me. I'm in a big hurry. Some other time, Monsieur Dièze, I'll see you later."

He pulled up, surprised by her reaction. My word, she was running away from him! Nevertheless, they'd been intimate enough that she should be willing to spend a few moments chatting with him.

And the child . . . What if it turned out that the child was his? He caught up with them again.

"Excuse me for insisting, but I'm eager to take advantage of this chance meeting. Would you like to have a cup of tea somewhere? Let's chat a bit."

It was the child who retained his mother. He looked up at Dièze and asked him if he could have a hot chocolate. "Of course, of course," he said. "Two even, if you want." Isabelle Faure sensed that she had lost the battle. The three of them set out for the nearest café.

Sitting at the table, they remained uncommunicative. Narcisse wondered why he'd been so insistent. After all, Mademoiselle Faure had not made any deep or lasting impression on him. It came down to the fact that Narcisse had wanted to display himself to her in his liberated state. To show himself off a little in his new life, in the presence of someone who'd known him only when he occupied a hospital bed.

Their beverages arrived, and still they weren't talking. The child was gazing at his hot chocolate and clasping the little spoon in his fist. Isabelle was staring down at the table.

Examining her more closely, Dièze found her rather pretty. And he had a desire to shine. To show himself at ease. Already integrated into the social fabric of the locality.

"You see, I've been definitively released from the psychiatric care unit. Totally cured. Wait, I'm going to show you something that will amaze you." He took his medical record from an inside pocket. He opened it to the page that spelled out the findings and handed it to her.

"Go ahead, read it. It will give me pleasure."

Isabel Faure let out a sigh of resignation and looked at the record before taking it. She read it quickly.

Dièze and the child exchanged glances.

"Well, it's very good," she said. "I wouldn't have believed the day would come when they'd let you leave. They didn't seem to understand your case very well."

She returned the booklet to him and looked him in the eye. That did the convalescent a world of good.

"What are you going to do now?"

"Right now, here? Spend a moment with you!"

He burst out laughing but stopped immediately, sensing that she wasn't as much at ease as he would have liked her to be.

Normal life wasn't so carefree after all. He put on a serious expression again, which was simple enough to do. He didn't really feel any desire to laugh. In fact, his eyes were tearing up now. He felt an urge to take out his box of pills. But not in front of Mademoiselle Faure. He took a swig of coffee. When he raised his eyes, she was looking at him with kindness.

As if she had accepted the idea of sharing a time with him.

"For the present, where will you be spending your days?"

"I don't really know about the days. In the evenings I'll return to the hospital. In a different department."

"So you aren't completely free?"

"No. Besides, all this has happened too fast for me, and I'll admit to you that I prefer this solution, this progression. But this evening, I'm invited to see my family."

"I never imagined you could have a family. On the contrary, I used to view you as an old orphan.

Narcisse felt himself blush.

Mademoiselle Faure clarified.

"For me, an orphan is a child. So I refer to a grown-up orphan as 'old.' I didn't mean to hurt your feelings."

There was a short silence.

"Are you married?"

She started laughing. She knew how to laugh.

"No. Don't you remember our understanding? I wanted to have and raise a child on my own. Well, this is Éric. Éric, this man is the one who helped me make you." Narcisse and Éric looked at each other. Narcisse was definitely the less surprised of the two.

"We have to go home now. Would you like to come with us? We live ten minutes from here."

They made the ten-minute walk in silence. Narcisse

felt his muscles tighten. His spinal column was losing its flexibility. He had trouble breathing. A crisis was impending. He had to hold on until they reached her apartment. At that point he could take a pill. Walking between them, the child took no interest in Narcisse. And Mademoiselle Faure seemed buried in deep thought.

Without the least embarrassment, Dièze requested a glass of water as soon as they arrived at the apartment. He had already taken out the pill and placed it on his tongue. She gave him the water.

"You might do well to take another. You don't look well."

Narcisse didn't have to be asked twice. After all, she was a nurse; she knew what was good for him.

"I'll leave you for a moment. I'm attending to my son. He needs to take a nap. Your job is to rest and relax."

Narcisse concentrated on his breathing. If he could breathe deeply, everything would go very well. But he could only manage to take in little gulps of air. He told himself it wouldn't take long for the pills to have an effect. He tried to relax his muscles, but it was as if he were paralyzed. Then a chill took hold of him. In his chest. The chill was gaining ground, and Narcisse was afraid of dying. For a short while. A minute or two. Then, the air seemed to flow in a bit more easily. He could breathe. The pills were taking effect, and Dièze was thankful for that. A little later, his muscles began slowly to loosen up. Stretched out on a sofa, he was recovering little by little. He certainly wasn't cured.

He got up and took a few steps. Mademoiselle Faure's apartment was small—three rooms, plausibly, but three tiny ones. He noticed a few attractive pieces of furniture and reflected that this was the first apartment he'd entered in seventeen years. That shocked him. All the more so because this apartment was also where his son lived.

"My son, Éric," he said out loud.

But that wasn't much more real than at the hospital when he was making love with the psychiatric care nurses or when he used to see them pregnant. Because he always told himself that they had someone else in their real lives and therefore he couldn't truly be sure of any paternity.

And even now. "I've seen my son," he told himself, yet those words had no substance. It was all too much for him to take in. He went to the window. He saw the street, other buildings, several windows, and it struck him that this was yet another vista—not the same as viewing the houses from the street. "I've seen so much on my first day out . . ."

Mademoiselle Faure returned. She was smiling. "He's sleeping, or pretending to," she said. "Excuse me for my earlier behavior, but it surprised me so much to see you that I didn't have time to decide if seeing you pleased me or not. Now I am pleased. Tell me about yourself."

"But you know my story well. Until this morning I was at the hospital. There's nothing that you couldn't imagine. Tell me instead how your life is now."

"You see it," she said, gesturing around the premises. "There's the apartment and Éric and my work. Right now I'm at the Diderot Hospital, and I've resumed my studies. I'm finishing a degree in psychology. Which won't benefit me at all, but which gives me the feeling of making better use of my time. I spend vacations at my parents' place. I have few friends. I live quietly. All the same, it's kind of a sad life at times.

"Do you have—I mean—is there a man in your life?"

"Absolutely! At times several men. But not often. And I don't miss that at all."

She paused to make him realize she'd say no more about this.

"Tell me about the family members you'll be visiting this evening. Are they closely related to you?"

"Oh! They're people I've known for a very long time. Yes, they are close, but I can't say I have familial feelings toward them. They're people who are doing me a service. It's thanks to them that I've been able to leave the hospital, since I had to have a sponsor on the outside."

Time was passing. Narcisse was feeling better and better, almost ecstatic. As he spoke, he was eying Isabelle Faure, looking her up and down. She was much prettier than he remembered. Sweeter, less overbearing. He suddenly felt so virile that he wanted to test whether this impression was well-founded. At a particular point, there was a lull in the conversation. Experiencing a visceral fear that she would reject him, feeling a tingling sensation from his fingers all the way to his shoulders, holding his breath, he approached her. His eyes fixed on Mademoiselle Faure's, Narcisse Dièze longed to seduce her. He knelt down near her and placed his hand on her thigh.

"What is it that you want, Monsieur Dièze?" she asked in a forbidding undertone that gave him the impression of being encased in a block of ice. He was about to search for the words to explain his desire when she told him in simple terms that she didn't desire him and that she would be pleased if he sat down again.

Which he did, of course, humiliated. Once more, his breathing came in small and jerky increments. He felt so uncomfortable that it was as if his body had swollen up. Sitting on the edge of his chair, he stammered an unintelligible sentence. Then he fainted.

The passage from a conscious state to an unconscious one had the gentleness of a slide into slumber. Narcisse experienced an inner relaxation. His extraordinary fainting spell in the presence of Mademoiselle Faure yielded abruptly to a strange state: it was as if his mind was beginning to live unconstrained and at its normal speed, which was lightning fast. He thought he'd entered the dying process, and it was in no way disagreeable. His mind was finally breaking free from his body, finally all-powerful, independent.

*

He woke up grudgingly, like at the hospital. Though he tried to fight it off, an unpleasant sensation was forcing him back into consciousness. An intense chill gripped his forehead. He stirred, but the sensation was still there, and he resigned himself to opening his eyes. Mademoiselle Faure was holding an icepack on his face. She looked pleased to see him wake up.

"You'll have to leave now. It's almost six o'clock, and you'll be meeting with your family soon. How are you feeling?"

"Queasy," he answered. He raised his head and glanced around. He was stretched out on the floor, and beneath his head was a cushion.

"I don't know what happened to me."

"You passed out. That can happen to someone who leaves the hospital after spending many years there."

"It seemed to me . . ."

"Yes, you must have misjudged your own feelings, but that happens, too. I recall a case that was similar to yours. The patient was living entirely in a world of his own, and he was imagining other people's reactions in terms of what he, and he alone, was feeling. For you, it seems to me that it's a transitory condition, a slight imbalance that you'll quickly get over."

Narcisse raised himself to a sitting position on the floor. Turning his head, he saw Éric, who seemed deep

in thought: he was looking at Narcisse with disconcert-
ing intensity.

Then, aided by Mademoiselle Faure, he stood up. He
drank the glass of water she handed him. He tried taking a few steps. He could walk. So, he said his goodbyes
and left the apartment.

The next hour went by without leaving any imprint
on Narcisse Dièze's memory. Nevertheless, as he was
ringing the doorbell at his relatives' house, he noticed
that he was carrying his suitcase. Therefore, he had
stopped in at the shop. He looked at his watch: it was
exactly seven. That kind of precision meant a lot to him.

Chapter 4

No sooner had Narcisse touched his finger to the doorbell than he wished he hadn't. He wasn't ready yet. But he heard a distant sound. His action had produced a result. He would have liked to run away, but that wasn't possible. So he stayed planted on the doorstep in a state of alarm as the steps from within drew closer. His breathing was unsteady; he regretted not taking a pill before going to the door. It was opened by a friendly-looking woman who asked him what he wanted. The only response Narcisse could make was to mutter his name. She swept open the door and invited him in.

Narcisse crept into the apartment with tiny steps, like a sick old man. Then he extended his hand and introduced himself again.

"Narcisse Dièze."

"I know, Monsieur. I'm Andrée."

She did not shake Narcisse's outstretched hand but

by a demonstrative gesture conveyed to him that she was waiting to take his coat. He blushed abruptly, as if all his inhibitions were registering on his face. He set down his suitcase and removed his raincoat. Andrée took it and went to hang it in a little coat closet. Already Narcisse was wondering how to dispose of his suitcase appropriately. Should he take hold of it again, leave it there, carry it to the coat closet? He chose the first solution and stood there motionless. Andrée came back, saying, "If you would follow me, please."

Tightly gripping the suitcase handle, Dièze followed on her heels. They moved through long, narrow corridors. The space was dimly lit. Sometimes they passed through small sitting rooms, situated at intervals like way stations. But still they didn't stop. He heard the sound of voices. People were conversing not far from him. Narcisse couldn't tell if they were speaking low to keep him from hearing their words or if it was simply the distance that muffled the voices. He switched his suitcase to his other hand and gave a little sigh.

"We're almost there," Andrée told him, turning around.

"Yes, yes," replied Dièze, caught out.

They continued along a curving corridor. The parquet floor was freshly waxed, and its smell revived an imprecise memory in Narcisse's mind. The woman halted in front of an open door.

"This is your room. A little farther along, you have

a bathroom on the right. I'll be back in about fifteen minutes to show you to the living room."

Dièze took a few steps into the room and set down his suitcase. It was an average-sized room with an unsettling sterility. Whoever had occupied the room before him had left hardly a trace.

Turning around, he noticed that the door had remained open. Dièze made a move to close it. But wasn't there a risk that Andrée would interpret his action as a sign of defiance? He solved the problem by leaving the room. Then he retraced his steps, since he'd forgotten his toiletries kit.

He went along the corridor. The bathroom door was open. The room was minuscule. Ancient. Like all that he had seen of the house. An antiquated bathtub wedged between the wall and the water heater. A sink, with a mirror above it. Two towels and two facecloths on the bathtub rim. Maybe those objects had been placed there for him, but Narcisse, unsure of that, disregarded them. After washing his hands and face, he dried off with his own towel, the one they gave him at the hospital. It had a comfortingly familiar smell.

He returned to his room and shut the door.

Fifteen minutes after leaving him, Andrée returned. Impressed by her punctuality, Narcisse followed her.

The closer he got to the living room, the clammier his hands felt to him. Droplets of sweat ran down from his underarms. His stomach let out a growl, which he covered after a slight delay by clearing his throat. The worst was still to come: before the last bend in the corridor, Narcisse Dièze sneezed. He hurriedly wiped his nose and hoped it was clean as he stuffed his handkerchief in his pocket. Andrée stopped to knock at a door, opened it and said, "This is the living room. Your whole family is here."

She stepped aside to let him past, and he entered. He took two steps and had the feeling of standing in contemplation of a painting. Men and women of different generations, all smiling. The men stood up. A man who seemed to be the oldest came toward Narcisse. He had a benevolent and diffident manner. He murmured a few words that were audible only because the ambient silence was absolute.

"Ah, so here is our young man. I'm pleased to see you."

He shook hands with Narcisse and, holding him by the elbow, led him off to introduce him to everyone present. Narcisse shook the hand of an elderly woman who had expected him to kiss it. Recognizing his lapse a little too late, he decided to kiss the hand of another old woman sitting near the first. Fortunately, it struck him that by favoring the second woman, he'd be slighting the first. Thus, he continued giving handshakes until he'd finished with—by his count—the twelve people

who had gathered. The old man had calmly reeled off
each one's name and the details of their kinship with
Narcisse.

They all seemed nice, and Dièze wondered why
they'd stayed out of touch with him for so long. The
timidity that had stifled him when he entered the living
room gave way to a sense of well-being. He was grateful
to all these people for allowing him to be one of them.

From then on, his relations with them became
smoother and even easy.

Dièze could not have said that they were happy to
see him again after so many years, nor could he have
said the contrary. There was a kind of lightheartedness
in the air, and everyone seemed attuned to it. Narcisse
had only to produce one or two witticisms on the sofa
where they had him sit, a glass of liquor in his hand, for
him to feel accepted by all. Family occasions like this
must not have been frequent, for everyone was giving
the impression of wanting to profit as much as possible
from this one. Several persons, as if intoxicated by a
sudden freedom, recounted juicy anecdotes about the
family's ups and downs during Narcisse's long hospital
stay. The little acts of pettiness, the jealousies, the lingering feuds—all of these became the pretext for indulgent
smiles, and a breeze of reconciliation wafted through
every head.

When the group moved to the table, a man
approached Dièze, took his arm, and asked him to

sit next to him. There was a momentary pause among those in attendance, like an impending resistance, and then everyone sat down around the table in no apparent order, and Narcisse sat beside the man. The dining room was an expansive space with a lofty ceiling, though it lacked character. The table took up a third of the room. No one pointed out that there were thirteen at the table. Before the conversations could resume, Andrée made her entry, holding an enormous soup tureen at the end of her outstretched arms. A boisterous exuberance erupted all around.

While two or three persons were recounting the family history, Narcisse examined them closely. He had difficulty imagining that he and they had something in common. Particular memories cropped up in his mind, however, and he readily pictured himself within the stories they told.

The family members ate abundantly and drank moderately, and Dièze felt good, as if released from a burden or mistake. Not knowing clearly what place he could claim in this family, he didn't dare open up without restraint. Instead, he launched into two stories about his life at the hospital, and he had good success with those. Satisfied, he spent the rest of the evening listening to others. The man who had wanted to sit beside him was one of the most reserved. He was a likable fellow, very thin, and you could imagine that he had a substantial inner life. He spoke little, but when he did, the others quieted down in order to listen to him. He didn't tell stories but instead made serious remarks about seemingly laughable situations. Like the others, Narcisse didn't quite know how to relate to him. He was able to ascertain that the man's name was Marc Labrèque and that he was the husband of Élisabeth, a pretty woman sitting across from Dièze.

During the course of the meal, Narcisse was able to scrutinize all of the individuals, one after another. Four generations were gathered, and he was trying to think: this one here is my cousin; that one over there, my uncle; next to him, my nephew; my sister, her husband, et cetera. He felt clearly that he used to be one of them in an earlier time, that he'd been brought up with them, and he was glad to see them again. But he wasn't sorry he had to leave again the following morning.

After the meal, they all returned to the living room. One of the cousins, feeling unwell, went to bed. It was late, and they drank champagne as they proffered good wishes for Narcisse's complete recovery. Labrèque, the family elder, even paid him a sort of little tribute in verse, which was a resounding success. As time went on, several guests took their leave. Narcisse wondered when it would be polite for him, in turn, to head off to bed. He found himself alone for a time with Marc and Élisabeth Labrèque, along with the latter's mother, Marie Chatenoud, a woman of infinite sweetness. Marc was resting his elbow on the mantle and smoking his pipe in a remarkably unhurried manner. Élisabeth was smiling, and her mind seemed elsewhere. Marc cleared his throat and said, "No doubt you hold a grudge against us for all those years of silence."

In a single movement, his wife and his mother-in-law glanced down at their shoes.

"No, of course not. Why?"

"We could have, we should have, come to see you. But we had our own set of problems here. You know what families are, and to tell you the whole truth, until recently we'd more or less forgotten you."

It was Narcisse's turn to start looking at his feet. He felt free to say what he was thinking.

"I don't resent you in any way. Things don't always happen the way we'd like. Besides, my illness has been a long slog, and I believe that being cut off from all of you has been beneficial to me. It would not have been easy for me to deal with certain problems if you'd been seeing me regularly. During that long period, I believe our interests—for different reasons—coincided."

The foursome looked at one another. Narcisse recalled his previous hard feelings and relinquished them in the presence of three persons of good will, bogged down in relationships they couldn't control.

Marc Labrèque came up to him and squeezed his shoulder in a gesture that Marc certainly intended as affectionate. Then he left the room, followed by the two women, who gave Narcisse little smiles as they left. The necessary words had been spoken.

That night, Narcisse Dièze fell into a leaden slumber and woke up with a strong desire to get away. He dressed quickly, stowed several items in his suitcase, and left his room. Following the route he'd taken the night before on Andrée's heels, he arrived at the dining room. No one was there. He opened a door that led into a little hallway. At the end of it was a kitchen. Narcisse went in. Again, no one was there. However, it was not so early that everyone would still be asleep: ten in the morning. What was especially surprising was the absence of noise. Like a house in a dream. Dièze set his suitcase in a corner and his raincoat on a chair. He wondered if he was permitted to have breakfast, but he swept aside any objection by telling himself that he was, after all, in his own family's house.

He then set himself the task of finding the ingredients needed to make a cup of coffee. Narcisse randomly opened the top cabinets and discovered stacks of plates, glasses, saucepans, one after the other. He took down one of the pans, went to fill it with water at the sink, set it on the stove. Next, he looked for two things: first of all, the gas knob, which he found very easily, and second, the matches. He looked where it was reasonable to assume they'd be kept, that is to say, near the stove. But he didn't find them. Things here obeyed a different logic. His eyes made a circuit of the room but failed to spot a box of matches anywhere. So, he began opening the various drawers, and it was in one of them that he found was he was after, amid the corkscrews, bottle openers, rubber bands, and a ball of string.

While the water was heating, Narcisse continued his search. The coffee was easy to find: it was in the mini fridge. A partially used packet clasped shut by two paper clips. Then, on a fairly high shelf, he saw a box of paper filters and a plastic cone. Only the coffee pot was missing. He searched with edgy impatience. "Where would they keep it?" Near the filters would have been a sensible place, but the evidence was clear: the coffee pot was nowhere near its accessories.

The water was boiling. When he opened the packet of coffee from the top of the fridge, Narcisse noticed that it contained coffee beans. Thus, he'd also have to find a coffee grinder. He turned off the burner under the pan.

Speaking out loud—he did so unwittingly—he asked himself the twofold question: "Where would a coffee grinder and a coffee pot be stored in this kitchen?" Simultaneously, he was opening all the lower cabinets. At the far end of the shelf where he'd found the filters, he discovered a hand-cranked coffee grinder and a carafe that could serve as a coffee pot.

Everything in this kitchen was modern, with the exception of the grinder. That made Narcisse smile as he sat down on a chair, wedged the grinder between his legs, opened the cover, filled the hopper with beans, and turned the crank. He told himself he was going to a lot of trouble for little benefit and that it would have been simpler to go and drink a coffee elsewhere. But since he'd begun, he might as well finish the job. When he opened the wooden drawer full of ground coffee, he felt a satisfaction that bore scant relation to the situation. The aroma of the coffee, the operation he had accomplished by himself, isolated in this house where he had, however, once lived—all of that put him in a buoyant mood.

He relit the gas under the saucepan, placed the plastic cone on the carafe, placed a paper filter in the cone, filled the filter with ground coffee, and waited for the water to come to a boil.

When it was time, Narcisse poured the boiling water slowly over the ground coffee and observed with pleasure the sludge-like mass that formed as the liquid dripped into the carafe.

Finally, Narcisse Dièze could drink his coffee in an outsized cup he'd found drying beside the sink. Ruling out any further activity in the kitchen, he drank it without sugar. The coffee tasted good to him.

Rapidly, he cleaned the items he had used, put the utensils back in their place, took his suitcase and raincoat, and left the house without encountering a soul.

All that day, Narcisse plied the city streets. He was obeying an imperative to stay in motion. It was essential for him to exhaust himself physically. He walked aimlessly, experiencing only the reality of his own movement. He paid almost no attention to others, concentrating entirely on his own progress. When he returned to the hospital that evening, he went to knock on Perrolaz's door. The professor was not alone. A woman was there, sitting in one of the armchairs facing the desk. Responding to Perrolaz's invitation, Narcisse sat down in the other chair and waited.

"Excuse me for a moment, Monsieur Dièze, I'm close to settling several details with this person."

Narcisse spread his hands to convey that he had plenty of time and settled into his chair. He wasn't listening to the conversation, he was beginning to feel the soreness in his limbs. Little by little, however, his fatigue made him drowsy. It was a pleasant sensation that Dièze couldn't remember experiencing before. He stretched out his legs, listened to his breathing. His mind was relaxing. He also felt an extraordinary absence of mental stress. His mind was floating in the room, and that produced a state of well-being. Lulled by the hum of the conversation, Dièze surrendered himself to a reverie.

He was very little and he was stretched out in a bathtub. The water was hot and he wanted to sleep. But it was dangerous to fall asleep there. So he was trying to straighten up, but his position was becoming uncomfortable. The gratification available to him was in an unstable equilibrium, bounded on the one hand by an absolute pleasure that would have brought him to ruin and on the other by a discomfort, an ache, that was preserving his life. Incapable of deciding, he alternated between one position and the other.

The dream was becoming impossible. He sat up straight in his chair and looked around. Perrolaz was scowling and must have refused something the woman wanted. She was trying one last time to win him over, but the professor's tone became increasingly brusque and abrasive. He showed his visitor to the door and put an end to her entreaties by closing it behind her. He then returned to his desk, sat down, and ran his hands over his face. To put him at ease, Dièze stared at the ceiling. When he lowered his gaze, Perrolaz was beaming at him. Narcisse felt good and began smiling back at the professor.

"I have the feeling that if I stop walking, I'll die," Narcisse blurted out.

"There may be reasons for that."

"If there are, I don't know them. But this feeling is rooted deep inside me. I've walked all day long."

". . ."

"At this rate, I'll never hold up. I can't spend my whole life roaming around the city."

"At some point very soon you may have an urge to do something else with your time."

"Yes, but for the moment, if I keep walking, that's not bad for me, is it?

"I can't give you a definite answer."

"Then what should I do tomorrow?"

"Do what you want, Monsieur Dièze. It's up to you to answer that question. At the moment, you're experiencing quite powerful impulses, and you must follow them until you develop the strength to put them in order. Don't be anxious. You look splendid."

"I'm afraid of falling apart."

"I don't think there's much chance of that."

"So, I should carry on?"

"You'll see for yourself, Narcisse," said Perrolaz as he stood up.

Dièze stood up in turn and let himself be guided to the door. The professor was holding him by the elbow as if to support him and at the same time nudge him out into the corridor.

"Try to relax. Let yourself go a little, and everything will be fine."

Narcisse felt vaguely uneasy. Perrolaz's responses were strangely detached.

"You're still looking out for me?"

"Of course, Monsieur Dièze, of course. Don't worry about a thing. Get some rest, sleep easy, and tomorrow, make the most of your day."

"Do you still want me to talk to you for your book?"

"I haven't changed my mind."

Narcisse was in the corridor now, and he sensed that the door was about to close. He still had something to say, but what? He swayed from one foot to the other, hesitating, stammering several disconnected phrases. And it was just as he found the words, just as he was opening his mouth to speak, that Perrolaz closed the door with extreme gentleness, saying in his deep baritone: "Good evening, Narcisse, good evening."

Narcisse was frustrated for a moment, like someone who'd just had the phone hung up on him. Then he erupted in anger toward the professor. If that was how it was going to be, then he wouldn't come to talk with Perrolaz anymore. And then he'd find out whether he was capable of writing his book by himself.

Dièze went down a flight of stairs to reach his minuscule room, promising along the way to make Perrolaz pay a heavy price for his indifference. He flung down his suitcase and raincoat on the bed. He went to the window and leaned his forehead against the pane.

Then he stormed out of the room and down the stairs, crossed the grounds, climbed two flights of stairs in another building, went down a corridor, and knocked on Mauméjean's office door. There was no answer. He knocked harder. No response. He shouted through the door: "It's me, Narcisse. Open up!"

But either the doctor refused to open the door to him or she wasn't in her office. So Dièze did something that in former times he'd have been unable to do: he tried to open the door without being invited in. To his great relief, it was locked. Thus, having exhausted every recourse, he could return to his room. Perrolaz had ejected him, Mauméjean was absent. He collapsed in his armchair, near the window, and realized then that he was drenched in sweat. He took his towel and bar of soap and went down the hall to the showers.

Narcisse woke up with a pasty mouth and a foggy mind. It was lovely outside, and he got dressed at a deliberate pace. Before going outside, he considered taking his raincoat. Not that he expected to need it as protection from a possible shower, but simply because it was reassuring to have a garment that provided a certain security.

He gave a fatalistic shrug and left the raincoat hanging on its hook.

Outside, a fresh breeze gradually relieved the migraine most likely provoked by the sleeping pills he'd taken to ensure a restful night.

People seemed less rushed than the day before, as if the pleasant weather was tempering their pace.

Narcisse went in search of a café where he could have breakfast. He ruled out many of them before making his choice.

He sat down at a sunlit sidewalk table.

Later, he made his way to a kiosk, bought a number of newspapers, and returned to sit at the sidewalk café.

He appreciated that, in addition to the coffees he was drinking, they brought him a glass of water he hadn't requested but was glad to have.

Another morning, at around eleven, Dièze decided to go and dine at a Chinese restaurant he'd seen. The heat was so strong that he carried his raincoat over his arm, feeling vaguely ridiculous. He awaited the lunch hour by strolling along one of the banks of the major river that flowed through the city. After several minutes, he saw a collection of tables and chairs set out on the bankside. "Funny place for a café," he thought. A man was sitting there with an empty cup in front of him. He was reading a newspaper. Narcisse had an impulse to stop there and at the same time a fear of doing so. A diffuse fear he'd known well since leaving the hospital. In fact, to be precise, what he felt was an uneasiness, no doubt provoked by the exposed outdoor location of this café.

He wanted to stop there, have a glass of wine, but at the same time, he didn't dare. On his first approach, he crossed through the space occupied by the tables and chairs and continued on his way. He was looking at the river. "Why," he asked himself, "can't I do what I want to do? There's no insurmountable obstacle. I sit down at a table, I set down my raincoat, and I adopt a relaxed demeanor while waiting for someone to come and take my order." He bristled with self-anger, made a U-turn, collided with a chair, resumed his advance, and sat down abruptly at a random table. His heart was pounding, and he was sweating profusely. He began counting in his head to give himself time to recover. Then his attention was attracted by the sound of a newspaper being crumpled. The man who was sitting several tables from him went away without taking his paper. Had he forgotten it? Had he left without paying? Narcisse, dumbfounded, felt that he was caught in a trap. Were they going to ask him to pay that man's bill? No, that was ridiculous. First of all, the man had undoubtedly paid for whatever he consumed: you don't skip out on a public establishment like that. Dièze forced himself to contemplate the river. He remained absorbed in it until he felt calmer and better prepared to confront the situation in store for him.

But no one came to take his order. He looked around to his left and his right: he was alone. The easiest solution would have been to leave. It was perfectly legitimate to leave a café where they fail to wait on you within a reasonable time. But Narcisse was thirsty and, more importantly, the place was intriguing to him. If he stayed seated as he was, something would surely happen. After all, someone had surely come to serve the other customer, since the cup was sitting there on the table. Therefore, he had only to wait.

After several more minutes, Dièze felt his annoyance mounting. But he definitely did not want to leave that place. To conceal his exasperation, he got up and went to claim the newspaper left by the previous customer.

Sitting back down at his own table, Narcisse Dièze felt excited about his daring seizure of something that didn't belong to him. His satisfaction was at the same level as the fear he'd felt of being caught in the act. He snickered slyly at his success.

At first, his vision was blurry. Little by little his eyes became accustomed to the printed words in the newspaper, and he was able to read them.

Narcisse read the newspaper through and through, from front to back. Fascinated by the stories and by their variety. Everything interested him, from politics to the economy, from general news to sports. But what fired his imagination the most were the miscellaneous news items. The brief accounts of lives turned upside down. He found it startling that so many people had difficulties with the real world. That woman who lived in a small apartment with two children. Everything was going normally for her: she worked in an office, her children went to school. But she couldn't bring herself to throw out the trash. The sanitation department, alerted by the neighbors, had discovered piles of trash everywhere, on top of the furniture, under the furniture. A kind of path was left clear to allow passage from one room to the next. Cockroaches and mice proliferated. To a person who asked her how she could stand living that way, she replied, "There's nothing to be done. At first, I tried using insecticides, but the bugs always come back."

Narcisse Dièze realized he'd lived for years according to the same reasoning.

The gravel crunched behind him. He turned around abruptly. A man of indeterminate age was advancing toward the table that had been occupied by the previous customer. He removed the cup and saucer and walked away.

"Monsieur!" called out Narcisse, spontaneously. The waiter turned.

"May I have a coffee?"

Narcisse's question ended in a quivering murmur.

"We don't open till noon," replied the waiter, with a backward glance.

"Oh, that's all right."

Dièze stood up, folded the newspaper as if it were his, and left the area.

To be sure, he hadn't succeeded, he hadn't gotten himself served. He had, however, spent a comfortable hour lounging in the open air.

"I haven't wasted my time," he told himself, half aloud. "I read a newspaper."

He tossed it into a wastepaper basket and headed for the Chinese restaurant at a slow pace, thinking back on that strange café, the news stories he'd read, and his sense of unease. Everything was becoming jumbled in his mind, and he was happy to see that he'd arrived. The restaurant had a fairly small red front, with

Chinese characters painted in green. Narcisse tried to look inside, but the opaque curtains prevented him from making out the interior. He would have to decide based on the exterior. Dièze pushed the door open and entered.

*

By the time he asked for the bill, Narcisse Dièze felt like another man. They had greeted him like a traveler gone astray. When he found himself the object of so much attention, he rediscovered something of the pleasure of living. Four of them came to advise him on the menu and ask him whether he was enjoying his meal. On realizing that he was the only diner in the restaurant, Narcisse might have felt ill at ease at being the focal point to such an extent. But, on the contrary, he flourished amid this genial entourage, speaking freely and offering a sometimes-subtle analysis of the various flavors in each dish he chose on his hosts' advice. They brought him a coffee, which had the effect of plunging him into a near-rapturous state. He paid the bill, which turned out to be quite modest, and left promising he would soon return and that he'd talk up the restaurant in the local area. On those words, someone who seemed to be in charge of the operation put in his hands a dozen or so cards imprinted with the restaurant's name, location, and phone number.

"Solely for reservations," said the proprietor, with a smile that Narcisse found charming.

"Naturally," he replied. He pocketed the cards, and as he left, he gave a farewell wave to everyone present.

Outside, the sun bore down on Narcisse, who quickly sought out a shaded sidewalk. He walked for a good fifteen minutes, his mind assuaged. Then, passing in front of a vintage Art Nouveau building, he smelled a strong chemical odor. He reversed course and read on a plaque: "Municipal Swimming Pool." Dièze climbed several steps and pushed the door open. There was a glassed-in booth on the right, where tickets were being sold, and on the left he saw the pool and the bathers. At this hour of the afternoon, the pool was by no means crowded. A few old people, a handful of youngsters, several adults. Suddenly, Narcisse wanted to share the experience of these people who, despite being lost in what seemed a strange dimension, looked happy and relaxed. Some of them were frolicking on the surface. But he had neither a swimsuit nor a towel. He headed for the ticket booth and tapped lightly on the glass. The attendant, engrossed in his newspaper, barely raised his head.

"Is it possible to rent a swimsuit and a towel?"

"Eight francs for the suit, four for the towel, and two for a little bar of soap."

"I'll just take the suit and the towel," Narcisse said.

The man sighed, got up from his seat and went to rummage in a closet, from which he got out two swimsuits for Narcisse to consider.

"See which one you like."

Although Dièze was not up to date on swimsuit fashions, the ones being offered to him seemed at first glance to be grossly outdated. He appraised them hesitantly. Would he shrink back, refuse this experience for aesthetic reasons? That would be foolish. He picked one at random. He took the towel the man handed him, paid the entrance fee, plus the charge for the suit and towel, and proceeded to the changing room.

In his cubicle, as he was carefully placing his clothes on the plastic hanger, he rather regretted his hastiness. When he put on the swimming trunks he'd rented, he felt vaguely ridiculous. Leaving the cubicle and passing his personal effects to the changing room attendant, he felt so embarrassed that he blushed horribly. He followed the signs: "To the Pool." He bent over to look at his feet, which seemed ludicrously pale to him. He arrived at the "mandatory showers" and grimaced. He stayed under the spray for a few seconds in keeping with the rules and went on to the pool. It was very hot in the pool area. Advancing toward the pool edge, Narcisse told himself that it would be good to immerse himself and then swim. He was about to descend through the shallow end when someone called out to him. He turned toward the voice that was addressing him.

"Don't you have a swim cap?"

Coming toward him was a swimming instructor, a man wearing a well-fitting swimsuit and a snug tee shirt. He didn't look hostile, which was somewhat reassuring to Narcisse. He mumbled that no, he had rented the suit and towel but that no one had told him he was required to wear a swim cap.

"Look around. Everybody has one."

To avoid giving the impression of doubting the instructor's word, Dièze hazarded only the briefest circular scan. And, in fact, everyone was wearing a swim cap, which contributed to the strange atmosphere that Narcisse was sensing.

"May I rent one of those, too? But I don't have any money on me," said Narcisse, showing that the rented towel was the only object he was carrying.

"Come with me," said the instructor, who turned around and went toward the employee locker room. "I'm going to lend you one for today, but if you come back, you'll have to get one of your own."

The man was speaking in a level, unruffled tone, and yet he had an authority that Narcisse would not for a moment have dreamed of challenging. The man handed him a blue swim cap.

When Dièze, after some difficulties, managed to put on the cap, which pinched his head somewhat, he had the impression that everyone would laugh at him. But they were all silently absorbed in their swimming routines. To his relief, no one was looking at him. He eased himself into the pool. It was on the cool side, and it gave off a whiff of chlorine. Narcisse launched himself forward and took several strokes. He was contented.

He tried swimming the crawl to focus his energy. After several meters, he inhaled a mouthful of water, spluttered, struggled to breathe normally. He felt himself on the verge of panic, and he lunged toward the edge. He could no longer breathe, he was coughing more and more violently, close to vomiting. His eyes were clouding over.

He was afraid he would die right there in that pool, with that ridiculous cap pinching his head. He needed a pill, but he'd left them in his jacket pocket in the changing area. Once he was able to breathe a little more regularly between bouts of coughing, he knew that this incident didn't amount to a crisis. He had merely choked after swallowing water. He was reassured, and, clinging to the pool edge with both hands, he waited to get his breath back.

Later, he tried a bit of breaststroke, swimming to the far end of the pool and returning to the shallow end. He sat back on his heels and watched the other swimmers. An elderly lady was beside him. "We're better off here than outside." Narcisse could only respond with a smile. He groped for a banal remark along the lines the lady was expecting. Not coming up with one, he settled for nodding vigorously to show his agreement. The lady moved away, swimming slowly and confidently. A young woman swimming on her back was approaching the low wall at the shallow end. She was going to bump her head unless Narcisse intervened. But how would it look if he started shouting, "Watch out, you're going to hit the wall!" The young woman might be offended. Maybe she knew exactly what she was doing. She was getting dangerously close to the wall. Narcisse turned away so as not to be responsible. He looked elsewhere.

It was only when he heard a thud that he turned back again in utter guilt, his stomach knotted, his nerves on edge. The young woman had stood up and was holding her head. She was briskly rubbing her scalp. She looked at Narcisse and started laughing.

"I need eyes in the back of my head!"

She was talking to him. She hadn't noticed his cowardice. Relieved, Narcisse reshaped his mouth in hopes of producing a smile and searched at top speed for a reply that would fit the situation. All that he could think of to say was, "Right! That would be useful."

She began swimming again. Always on her back, which attested to an admirable perseverance. Narcisse wanted to leave immediately, but he made a point of calmly executing a few laps without looking at the other swimmers. He felt a sort of numbness coming over his body. It was a surprisingly pleasant feeling. He even felt a kind of harmony between the motion of his arms and that of his legs. As if he were finding an equilibrium, without looking for it, between his breathing and his limbs.

Dièze stayed in the water for another thirty minutes and then left the pool area.

He went straight back to the hospital, stretched out on his bed, and stared at the ceiling. Narcisse Dièze felt as empty as ever. He'd spent a day outside without a disabling panic attack, doing what all the others did, the usual things, and yet he still felt less than whole. To tell the truth, he was close to letting out a sigh, as he used to in earlier times, when, as an adolescent, he pondered the meaning of life.

Nonchalantly, without anxiety, he invited the person knocking on his door to enter. He tensed barely, if at all, when he recognized Perrolaz. But he didn't budge. The professor hesitated over what demeanor to adopt. He didn't take long to choose the worst: joviality.

"So, Narcisse, are you giving me the brush-off? It's been a while since you came to see me."
He moved closer to the bed and sat down on the armchair without being invited.
"You're tired, for sure. That's understandable. What did you do today?"

Narcisse Dièze sat up on his bed, swung his legs over,

and found himself standing. Propping his back against the wall, he eyed his visitor.

"Not a whole lot. The time went by."

"Yes, certainly. You can't expect to be instantly integrated into society. Would you like me to introduce you to a person who was cured of the same illness as you and who now leads a normal life?"

"I don't think so."

Perrolaz was thrown off balance, that was obvious. Dièze stuck firmly to his position and could hardly believe it. He was the way he yearned to be, he was fearlessly standing up to his visitor. And when Perrolaz got to his feet with a nervous smile, Narcisse had the feeling of carrying off a tremendous victory.

"Listen, I think for the time being you should shape your experiences all by yourself. For that reason, it's probably too early for you to meet other former patients who've reintegrated."

With some regret, the professor made for the door. He was fumbling for a final optimistic remark to maintain a consistency between his entry and his departure, but he found nothing to say. Right by the door, he flashed his trademark magnificent smile and winked at Narcisse.

"Of course, you'll come see me when you want."

Chapter 5

Dièze became acquainted with a group of actors in a café he frequented. Absorbed in reading his newspapers, he would sometimes hear a babble behind him. He enjoyed sensing the presence of others, the conversations from table to table. There were young people dressed eccentrically, as well as older, calmer individuals, all of them chattering as if their lives depended on it. At first, Narcisse would listen to the people speaking, but then, since he had no idea what they were discussing, he'd shift around in his seat and concentrate on his reading.

One afternoon, the discussions were so heated that the lines of his newspaper began dancing before his eyes. Annoyed, he turned around. He said something like, "Please! Less noise"—not ill-naturedly, but with a firmness he came close to regretting.

"After all," he thought, "it's true that they're making a hell of a racket."

He was about to resume his reading when he heard someone calling to him. "Monsieur!" He turned around. "May we ask a favor of you?" Oh, boy! thought Dièze, feeling a drop of sweat trickle down his spine. What is it now?

"Of course," he said.

"Here's the thing: we're doing a run-through of our play at five o'clock, and we'd like to have the opinion of someone who isn't connected with theater. Would you be able to attend?"

It seemed to Narcisse that the person addressing him was the leader of the acting troupe. He was secretly flattered by that.

"A run-through?"

"A final rehearsal where we act out the whole play with no interruptions."

"And so?"

"So we'd like you to give us your opinion."

"I know nothing about theater."

"Exactly. You'll give us a random audience member's opinion. That would be a big help to us, you know."

"Ah, I see. All right. I'd like to do that. Yes."

Noticing that Narcisse was flustered, the leader got up and led his group out of the room.

"See you soon," he said to Narcisse.

"Yes," replied Narcisse.

Somewhat flabbergasted, Narcisse found himself alone with his newspapers. But he couldn't manage to read them. He was proud and pleased that the actors had approached him and, needless to say, anxious about being asked for his opinion.

*

Narcisse Dièze became friends with the acting troupe. After the rehearsal, they handed him an invitation to the premiere. He took it respectfully and was choked with emotion when he noticed that the invitation was valid for two people. Who could he invite, then? Does anyone ever go alone to a premiere?

The play enjoyed a measure of success, and little by little Narcisse became part of the group. Recognizing that he had free time, the actors entrusted him with a few technical tasks, which, to his great surprise, he carried out satisfactorily. He even replaced the manager for a day. Luck played a part, and everything worked out well.

In the aftermath of a falling-out, the ticket seller ran off with an actor's wife. Behind the scenes, the troupe was thrown into disarray. Quite naturally, they asked Narcisse to handle the ticket sales. This time he balked. He couldn't imagine being able to make change without getting things wrong. But they astutely pointed out to him that someone had to take on the job and that nobody else was available. That Narcisse should do his best and everything would go well.

"But what if I make a mistake?"

"So you'll make a mistake!"

"And you'll take it as lightly as that?"

"The last cashier made more than his share of mistakes."

Reassured on that score, Narcisse once again played his part.

Months went by. Dièze meshed with the group more and more easily. He was discovering the security, the well-being, that came from a regular job. He liked the fact that the duties were varied.

*

Narcisse saw Perrolaz less and less. That didn't seem to bother the professor, and their chance encounters on the stairs, in the elevator, or in the corridor had the bland coloration of urban routine.

Narcisse was living his life on his own terms. He no longer saw Mauméjean, and that saddened him at times. But, he said to himself, life is like that!

*

One day he was offered a half-time salary for continuing to work with the troupe. He was going to earn some money. He received his first paycheck. He was one of the "others."

*

And they offered him a part.

And once again Narcisse Dièze accepted. He couldn't be more incompetent in that job than in the others. Besides, he had nothing to lose.

*

He discovered he had a good memory when he had to learn a fairly long script. They told him that he "moved well." Whatever they told him, he took as it came. Here, as elsewhere. Narcisse was looking to do well.

*

The performance was at the point where Narcisse had to take his first steps. He came forward. To some degree, he still had the freedom to speed up or slow down his pace.

Thus, he felt free. The heat and the stage lights didn't bother him. He was going to speak his lines, and that afforded Narcisse a moment of pleasure. He knew that his voice would ring true now. He held back on his first line for a couple of seconds. He felt the audience's attention, and his comrades'. He was attuned to the regular rhythm of his breathing.

Then Narcisse recited his first line.

"Was I so far away? You speak of me like a dead person."

And the rest flowed from one line to the next. All of it. Dièze was no longer afraid of forgetting his lines. He knew that by listening for the cues from his fellow actors and speaking his lines at just the right moments, he would never fumble for words.

The performance ended with a song sung by the actors who were on stage for the final scene. There were four of them. Narcisse had to sing last, solo, out of sync, as if to call attention to himself.

And every evening, at that precise moment, a memory came to him of another song, another place.

He wasn't quite five. It was during the school gala, and his parents weren't present. He was singing *Gentil coquelicot* with his class. Little by little, the others had trailed off. But Dièze knew all the rhymed verses by heart and saw no reason to stop before the song was over.

He remembered his voice that day, timid yet persistent. His schoolmates and their parents had laughed at his doggedness. But Narcisse Dièze had carried on to the end.

FINIS

May 1988

MICHAL AJVAZ, *The Golden Age.*
The Other City.

PIERRE ALBERT-BIROT, *Grabinoulor.*

YUZ ALESHKOVSKY, *Kangaroo.*

FELIPE ALFAU, *Chromos.*
Locos.

JOE AMATO, *Samuel Taylor's Last Night.*

IVAN ÂNGELO, *The Celebration.*
The Tower of Glass.

ANTÓNIO LOBO ANTUNES, *Knowledge of Hell.*
The Splendor of Portugal.

ALAIN ARIAS-MISSON, *Theatre of Incest.*

JOHN ASHBERY & JAMES SCHUYLER, *A Nest of Ninnies.*

ROBERT ASHLEY, *Perfect Lives.*

GABRIELA AVIGUR-ROTEM, *Heatwave and Crazy Birds.*

DJUNA BARNES, *Ladies Almanack.*
Ryder.

JOHN BARTH, *Letters.*
Sabbatical.

DONALD BARTHELME, *The King.*
Paradise.

SVETISLAV BASARA, *Chinese Letter.*

MIQUEL BAUÇÀ, *The Siege in the Room.*

RENÉ BELLETTO, *Dying.*

MAREK BIENCZYK, *Transparency.*

ANDREI BITOV, *Pushkin House.*

ANDREJ BLATNIK, *You Do Understand.*
Law of Desire.

LOUIS PAUL BOON, *Chapel Road.*
My Little War.
Summer in Termuren.

ROGER BOYLAN, *Killoyle.*

IGNÁCIO DE LOYOLA BRANDÃO, *Anonymous Celebrity.*
Zero.

BONNIE BREMSER, *Troia: Mexican Memoirs.*

CHRISTINE BROOKE-ROSE, *Amalgamemnon.*

BRIGID BROPHY, *In Transit.*
The Prancing Novelist.

GERALD L. BRUNS, *Modern Poetry and the Idea of Language.*

GABRIELLE BURTON, *Heartbreak Hotel.*

MICHEL BUTOR, *Degrees.*
Mobile.

G. CABRERA INFANTE, *Infante's Inferno.*
Three Trapped Tigers.

JULIETA CAMPOS, *The Fear of Losing Eurydice.*

ANNE CARSON, *Eros the Bittersweet.*

ORLY CASTEL-BLOOM, *Dolly City.*

LOUIS-FERDINAND CÉLINE, *North.*
Conversations with Professor Y.
London Bridge.

MARIE CHAIX, *The Laurels of Lake Constance.*

HUGO CHARTERIS, *The Tide Is Right.*

ERIC CHEVILLARD, *Demolishing Nisard.*
The Author and Me.

MARC CHOLODENKO, *Mordechai Schamz.*

JOSHUA COHEN, *Witz.*

EMILY HOLMES COLEMAN, *The Shutter of Snow.*

ERIC CHEVILLARD, *The Author and Me.*

ROBERT COOVER, *A Night at the Movies.*

STANLEY CRAWFORD, *Log of the S.S. The Mrs Unguentine.*
Some Instructions to My Wife.

RENÉ CREVEL, *Putting My Foot in It.*

RALPH CUSACK, *Cadenza.*

NICHOLAS DELBANCO, *Sherbrookes.*
The Count of Concord.

NIGEL DENNIS, *Cards of Identity.*

PETER DIMOCK, *A Short Rhetoric for Leaving the Family.*

ARIEL DORFMAN, *Konfidenz.*

COLEMAN DOWELL, *Island People.*
Too Much Flesh and Jabez.

ARKADII DRAGOMOSHCHENKO, *Dust.*

RIKKI DUCORNET, *Phosphor in Dreamland.*
The Complete Butcher's Tales.

FOR A FULL LIST OF PUBLICATIONS, VISIT: www.dalkeyarchive.com

RIKKI DUCORNET (cont.), *The Jade Cabinet*.
The Fountains of Neptune.

WILLIAM EASTLAKE, *The Bamboo Bed*.
Castle Keep.
Lyric of the Circle Heart.

JEAN ECHENOZ, *Chopin's Move*.

STANLEY ELKIN, *A Bad Man*.
Criers and Kibitzers, Kibitzers and Criers.
The Dick Gibson Show.
The Franchiser.
The Living End.
Mrs. Ted Bliss.

FRANÇOIS EMMANUEL, *Invitation to a Voyage*.

PAUL EMOND, *The Dance of a Sham*.

SALVADOR ESPRIU, *Ariadne in the Grotesque Labyrinth*.

LESLIE A. FIEDLER, *Love and Death in the American Novel*.

JUAN FILLOY, *Op Oloop*.

ANDY FITCH, *Pop Poetics*.

GUSTAVE FLAUBERT, *Bouvard and Pécuchet*.

KASS FLEISHER, *Talking out of School*.

JON FOSSE, *Aliss at the Fire*.
Melancholy.

FORD MADOX FORD, *The March of Literature*.

MAX FRISCH, *I'm Not Stiller*.
Man in the Holocene.

CARLOS FUENTES, *Christopher Unborn*.
Distant Relations.
Terra Nostra.
Where the Air Is Clear.

TAKEHIKO FUKUNAGA, *Flowers of Grass*.

WILLIAM GADDIS, JR., *The Recognitions*.

JANICE GALLOWAY, *Foreign Parts*.
The Trick Is to Keep Breathing.

WILLIAM H. GASS, *Life Sentences*.
The Tunnel.
The World Within the Word.
Willie Masters' Lonesome Wife.

GÉRARD GAVARRY, *Hoppla! 1 2 3*.

ETIENNE GILSON, *The Arts of the Beautiful*.
Forms and Substances in the Arts.

C. S. GISCOMBE, *Giscome Road*.
Here.

DOUGLAS GLOVER, *Bad News of the Heart*.

WITOLD GOMBROWICZ, *A Kind of Testament*.

PAULO EMÍLIO SALES GOMES, *P's Three Women*.

GEORGI GOSPODINOV, *Natural Novel*.

JUAN GOYTISOLO, *Count Julian*.
Juan the Landless.
Makbara.
Marks of Identity.

HENRY GREEN, *Blindness*.
Concluding.
Doting.
Nothing.

JACK GREEN, *Fire the Bastards!*

JIŘÍ GRUŠA, *The Questionnaire*.

MELA HARTWIG, *Am I a Redundant Human Being?*

JOHN HAWKES, *The Passion Artist*.
Whistlejacket.

ELIZABETH HEIGHWAY, ED., *Contemporary Georgian Fiction*.

AIDAN HIGGINS, *Balcony of Europe*.
Blind Man's Bluff.
Bornholm Night-Ferry.
Langrishe, Go Down.
Scenes from a Receding Past.

KEIZO HINO, *Isle of Dreams*.

KAZUSHI HOSAKA, *Plainsong*.

ALDOUS HUXLEY, *Antic Hay*.
Point Counter Point.
Those Barren Leaves.
Time Must Have a Stop.

NAOYUKI II, *The Shadow of a Blue Cat*.

DRAGO JANČAR, *The Tree with No Name*.

MIKHEIL JAVAKHISHVILI, *Kvachi*.

GERT JONKE, *The Distant Sound*.
Homage to Czerny.
The System of Vienna.

FOR A FULL LIST OF PUBLICATIONS, VISIT: www.dalkeyarchive.com

JACQUES JOUET, *Mountain R.*
Savage.
Upstaged.

MIEKO KANAI, *The Word Book.*

YORAM KANIUK, *Life on Sandpaper.*

ZURAB KARUMIDZE, *Dagny.*

JOHN KELLY, *From Out of the City.*

HUGH KENNER, *Flaubert, Joyce
and Beckett: The Stoic Comedians.*
Joyce's Voices.

DANILO KIŠ, *The Attic.*
The Lute and the Scars.
Psalm 44.
A Tomb for Boris Davidovich.

ANITA KONKKA, *A Fool's Paradise.*

GEORGE KONRÁD, *The City Builder.*

TADEUSZ KONWICKI, *A Minor
Apocalypse.*
The Polish Complex.

ANNA KORDZAIA-SAMADASHVILI,
Me, Margarita.

MENIS KOUMANDAREAS, *Koula.*

ELAINE KRAF, *The Princess of 72nd Street.*

JIM KRUSOE, *Iceland.*

AYSE KULIN, *Farewell: A Mansion in
Occupied Istanbul.*

EMILIO LASCANO TEGUI, *On Elegance
While Sleeping.*

ERIC LAURRENT, *Do Not Touch.*

VIOLETTE LEDUC, *La Bâtarde.*

EDOUARD LEVÉ, *Autoportrait.*
Newspaper.
Suicide.
Works.

MARIO LEVI, *Istanbul Was a Fairy Tale.*

DEBORAH LEVY, *Billy and Girl.*

JOSÉ LEZAMA LIMA, *Paradiso.*

ROSA LIKSOM, *Dark Paradise.*

OSMAN LINS, *Avalovara.*
The Queen of the Prisons of Greece.

FLORIAN LIPUŠ, *The Errors of Young Tjaž.*

GORDON LISH, *Peru.*

ALF MACLOCHLAINN, *Out of Focus.*
Past Habitual.

The Corpus in the Library.

RON LOEWINSOHN, *Magnetic Field(s).*

YURI LOTMAN, *Non-Memoirs.*

D. KEITH MANO, *Take Five.*

MINA LOY, *Stories and Essays of Mina Loy.*

MICHELINE AHARONIAN MARCOM,
A Brief History of Yes.
The Mirror in the Well.

BEN MARCUS, *The Age of Wire and String.*

WALLACE MARKFIELD, *Teitlebaum's
Window.*

DAVID MARKSON, *Reader's Block.*
Wittgenstein's Mistress.

CAROLE MASO, *AVA.*

HISAKI MATSUURA, *Triangle.*

LADISLAV MATEJKA & KRYSTYNA
POMORSKA, EDS., *Readings in Russian
Poetics: Formalist & Structuralist Views.*

HARRY MATHEWS, *Cigarettes.*
The Conversions.
The Human Country.
The Journalist.
My Life in CIA.
Singular Pleasures.
The Sinking of the Odradek.
Stadium.
Tlooth.

HISAKI MATSUURA, *Triangle.*

DONAL MCLAUGHLIN, *beheading the
virgin mary, and other stories.*

JOSEPH MCELROY, *Night Soul and
Other Stories.*

ABDELWAHAB MEDDEB, *Talismano.*

GERHARD MEIER, *Isle of the Dead.*

HERMAN MELVILLE, *The Confidence-
Man.*

AMANDA MICHALOPOULOU, *I'd Like.*

STEVEN MILLHAUSER, *The Barnum
Museum.*
In the Penny Arcade.

RALPH J. MILLS, JR., *Essays on Poetry.*

MOMUS, *The Book of Jokes.*

CHRISTINE MONTALBETTI, *The Origin
of Man.*
Western.

FOR A FULL LIST OF PUBLICATIONS, VISIT: www.dalkeyarchive.com

NICHOLAS MOSLEY, *Accident.*
Assassins.
Catastrophe Practice.
A Garden of Trees.
Hopeful Monsters.
Imago Bird.
Inventing God.
Look at the Dark.
Metamorphosis.
Natalie Natalia.
Serpent.

WARREN MOTTE, *Fables of the Novel:*
French Fiction since 1990.
Fiction Now: The French Novel in the
21st Century.
Mirror Gazing.
Oulipo: A Primer of Potential Literature.

GERALD MURNANE, *Barley Patch.*
Inland.

YVES NAVARRE, *Our Share of Time.*
Sweet Tooth.

DOROTHY NELSON, *In Night's City.*
Tar and Feathers.

ESHKOL NEVO, *Homesick.*

WILFRIDO D. NOLLEDO, *But for*
the Lovers.

BORIS A. NOVAK, *The Master of*
Insomnia.

FLANN O'BRIEN, *At Swim-Two-Birds.*
The Best of Myles.
The Dalkey Archive.
The Hard Life.
The Poor Mouth.
The Third Policeman.

CLAUDE OLLIER, *The Mise-en-Scène.*
Wert and the Life Without End.

PATRIK OUŘEDNÍK, *Europeana.*
The Opportune Moment, 1855.

BORIS PAHOR, *Necropolis.*

FERNANDO DEL PASO, *News from*
the Empire.
Palinuro of Mexico.

ROBERT PINGET, *The Inquisitory.*
Mahu or The Material.
Trio.

MANUEL PUIG, *Betrayed by Rita*
Hayworth.

The Buenos Aires Affair.
Heartbreak Tango.

RAYMOND QUENEAU, *The Last Days.*
Odile.
Pierrot Mon Ami.
Saint Glinglin.

ANN QUIN, *Berg.*
Passages.
Three.
Tripticks.

ISHMAEL REED, *The Free-Lance*
Pallbearers.
The Last Days of Louisiana Red.
Ishmael Reed: The Plays.
Juice!
The Terrible Threes.
The Terrible Twos.
Yellow Back Radio Broke-Down.

JASIA REICHARDT, *15 Journeys Warsaw*
to London.

JOÃO UBALDO RIBEIRO, *House of the*
Fortunate Buddhas.

JEAN RICARDOU, *Place Names.*

RAINER MARIA RILKE,
The Notebooks of Malte Laurids Brigge.

JULIÁN RÍOS, *The House of Ulysses.*
Larva: A Midsummer Night's Babel.
Poundemonium.

ALAIN ROBBE-GRILLET, *Project for a*
Revolution in New York.
A Sentimental Novel.

AUGUSTO ROA BASTOS, *I the Supreme.*

DANIËL ROBBERECHTS, *Arriving in*
Avignon.

JEAN ROLIN, *The Explosion of the*
Radiator Hose.

OLIVIER ROLIN, *Hotel Crystal.*

ALIX CLEO ROUBAUD, *Alix's Journal.*

JACQUES ROUBAUD, *The Form of*
a City Changes Faster, Alas, Than the
Human Heart.
The Great Fire of London.
Hortense in Exile.
Hortense Is Abducted.
Mathematics: The Plurality of Worlds of
Lewis.
Some Thing Black.

RAYMOND ROUSSEL, *Impressions of Africa.*

VEDRANA RUDAN, *Night.*

PABLO M. RUIZ, *Four Cold Chapters on the Possibility of Literature.*

GERMAN SADULAEV, *The Maya Pill.*

TOMAŽ ŠALAMUN, *Soy Realidad.*

LYDIE SALVAYRE, *The Company of Ghosts.*
The Lecture.
The Power of Flies.

LUIS RAFAEL SÁNCHEZ, *Macho Camacho's Beat.*

SEVERO SARDUY, *Cobra & Maitreya.*

NATHALIE SARRAUTE, *Do You Hear Them?*
Martereau.
The Planetarium.

STIG SÆTERBAKKEN, *Siamese.*
Self-Control.
Through the Night.

ARNO SCHMIDT, *Collected Novellas.*
Collected Stories.
Nobodaddy's Children.
Two Novels.

ASAF SCHURR, *Motti.*

GAIL SCOTT, *My Paris.*

DAMION SEARLS, *What We Were Doing and Where We Were Going.*

JUNE AKERS SEESE,
Is This What Other Women Feel Too?

BERNARD SHARE, *Inish.*
Transit.

VIKTOR SHKLOVSKY, *Bowstring.*
Literature and Cinematography.
Theory of Prose.
Third Factory.
Zoo, or Letters Not about Love.

PIERRE SINIAC, *The Collaborators.*

KJERSTI A. SKOMSVOLD,
The Faster I Walk, the Smaller I Am.

JOSEF ŠKVORECKÝ, *The Engineer of Human Souls.*

GILBERT SORRENTINO, *Aberration of Starlight.*
Blue Pastoral.
Crystal Vision.

Imaginative Qualities of Actual Things.
Mulligan Stew. Red the Fiend.
Steelwork.
Under the Shadow.

MARKO SOSIČ, *Ballerina, Ballerina.*

ANDRZEJ STASIUK, *Dukla.*
Fado.

GERTRUDE STEIN, *The Making of Americans.*
A Novel of Thank You.

LARS SVENDSEN, *A Philosophy of Evil.*

PIOTR SZEWC, *Annihilation.*

GONÇALO M. TAVARES, *A Man: Klaus Klump.*
Jerusalem.
Learning to Pray in the Age of Technique.

LUCIAN DAN TEODOROVICI,
Our Circus Presents...

NIKANOR TERATOLOGEN, *Assisted Living.*

STEFAN THEMERSON, *Hobson's Island.*
The Mystery of the Sardine.
Tom Harris.

TAEKO TOMIOKA, *Building Waves.*

JOHN TOOMEY, *Sleepwalker.*

DUMITRU TSEPENEAG, *Hotel Europa.*
The Necessary Marriage.
Pigeon Post.
Vain Art of the Fugue.

ESTHER TUSQUETS, *Stranded.*

DUBRAVKA UGRESIC, *Lend Me Your Character.*
Thank You for Not Reading.

TOR ULVEN, *Replacement.*

MATI UNT, *Brecht at Night.*
Diary of a Blood Donor.
Things in the Night.

ÁLVARO URIBE & OLIVIA SEARS, EDS.,
Best of Contemporary Mexican Fiction.

ELOY URROZ, *Friction.*
The Obstacles.

LUISA VALENZUELA, *Dark Desires and the Others.*
He Who Searches.

PAUL VERHAEGHEN, *Omega Minor.*

BORIS VIAN, *Heartsnatcher.*

AND MORE . . .